I0771268

RAINBOW RUN

John F. Carr
&
Camden Benares

Pequod Press

RAINBOW RUN
A Pequod Press Speculative Fiction Novel

First Edition

Manufactured in the United States of America
First Printing 2012

V 10 9 8 7 6 5 4 3 2 1

ISBN: 978-0-937912-24-9

On the cover: Alan Gutierrez, Rainbow Run
(*www.alangutierrez.com*)

Pequod Press
P.O. Box 80
Boalsburg, PA 16827
www.PequodPress.com

Novels by John F. Carr

Rainbow Run (with Camden Benares)
Gunpowder God
Space Viking's Throne (with Mike Robertson)
The Last Space Viking (with Mike Robertson)
Time Crime (with H. Beam Piper)
The Fireseed Wars
War World: The Battle of Sauron (with Don Hawthorne)
Siege of Tarr-Hostigos
Kalvan Kingmaker
Great Kings' War (with Roland Green)
Carnifex Mardi Gras
Pain Gain
The Ophidian Conspiracy

DEDICATION

To the memory of my best friend and brother-in-spirit, Camden Benares. R.I.P.

ONE

"Wake up or die!"

Those words hammered inside my skull, bounced back and forth, destroyed a fuzzy oblivion, and brought a reluctant return to consciousness.

Awareness came with a rush of pain—pounding head, burning stomach, aching muscles and stiff joints. I wasn't ready to open my eyes yet; all my energy was focused on holding still in an effort to minimize pain. I made an anguished attempt to recall what had happened to make me feel as if I were dying. I couldn't remember anything, not where I was—not even my name.

"Wake up or die!"

The shout hurt my ears. I opened my eyes. I was lying face down on a ledge that was higher than the tiled floor before me. I felt movement behind me—so slow and steady that I hadn't noticed it before. The wall behind me was moving, pushing me slowly toward the tiled floor. My left hand was hanging over the edge of the ledge, resting on one of the floor tiles.

Abruptly that tile dropped as if it had been held in place by an electronic magnet that lost power. My hand fell into the hole where the tile had been. I felt a pain in my palm as it touched the edge of a tile next to the hole. I yanked back my hand and saw a thin line of blood. The tile edges were razor sharp. I looked across the tiled floor and saw a lot of holes, all potential sources of dangerous cuts.

The only other person around was a woman, dressed like me in a brown tunic and sandals in the middle of the room, who was jumping from tile to tile to avoid the holes.

I cried out, "Thanks for the warning."

She glanced at me. Her face was unfamiliar.

She yelled, "Don't talk! Watch the tiles. Find the pattern. Get the rhythm. Get to that door and jump through it when it opens. It's the only way out. I'll see you in the winner's circle."

I looked at the door she had pointed to. Next to it was a display like an electronic scoreboard that showed a rainbow with some numbers beneath it:

$$1\ 2\ 7$$
$$-9\ 3$$
$$-6\ 1.$$

The numbers glowed. The door opened. The violet and orange tiles disappeared. By the time I'd taken several long, deep breaths the door had closed, the numbers on the display had changed, the missing tiles snapped back into position, and two more colors of tiles disappeared.

I could feel the wall behind me as it kept up its slow forward movement that was going to push me off the ledge and onto the tiles. I followed the woman's advice. I watched the tiles and looked for patterns. I looked at the numbers on the display. The three numbers in the first row hadn't changed but the two pairs of numbers in the other two rows were now different.

There were seven numbers. I counted the number of different colors among the tiles. There were seven: red, orange, yellow, green, blue, indigo, and violet—the colors of the rainbow. Could there be one number for each color? Was that the significance of the numbers?

There was a pattern to what was happening. Momentarily all the tiles would be in place and the door would open. Right after that, the numbers on the display would change and all the tiles of two colors would drop away. Within a short period of time the door would close and the tiles would reappear. Then the process would repeat.

I watched the woman hop forward, getting closer to the door. She put her right foot on a blue tile. The tile collapsed. Her leg disappeared into the hole, all the way up to her thigh. Before she could scramble out, the tiles closed again. Her leg was amputated; blood was spurting from the stump with every beat of her heart. She had severed her femoral artery and was bleeding to death.

I yelled, "Press down on your thigh! Stop the blood flow!"

I don't know if she heard me. She moaned as she crawled toward the door, bleeding profusely over the tiles.

All the tiles were back in place now. I wanted to help her. She had warned me, possibly saved my life. I didn't know if there would be time for me to get to her before the next two colors of tiles collapsed. I called out, "Use your hands to stop the blood flow."

I moved forward, but stopped suddenly when six tiles in front of me collapsed creating a hole the size of a grave. There was no way I could advance without falling in.

The moaning stopped. The woman was no longer crawling. She lay flat on the tiles that were as bloody as her tunic. No blood pulsed from her leg now; her heart had stopped. I couldn't save her now—no one could. It was too late.

I cautiously made my way back to the safety of the ledge. The wall was still moving forward, shrinking the size of the ledge. Soon there wouldn't be enough room to stand and I'd be forced back onto the dangerous tiles. I had to find the relationship between the numbers on the display and the disappearing tiles. If I didn't, I'd die here in this nightmare room. I looked at the display:

$$1\ 2\ 7$$
$$-6\ 0$$
$$-8\ 2.$$

The top three numbers hadn't changed. The other two pairs of numbers must identify what two colors of tiles that would collapse next. I added each of the pairs together, hoping the sums would identify the colors of the collapsing tiles. When that didn't work, I tried adding them in different combinations that led me nowhere. I tried subtraction. When I had subtracted and added every possible combination of both pairs and the three constant numbers in the display, I turned to multiplication and division but I found no meaningful results.

The numbers could represent an equation. The top three numbers were always constant. If they were the equation—probably a degree two equation with one number constant and the other two coefficients—then the lower pairs would be the variables. If I could determine the right equation and if each tile color was represented by only one number, I could solve the equation twice—once for each pair of numbers—and determine which two tile colors would drop out next. Then I could move toward the door and escape.

I studied the display:

$$1\ 2\ 7$$
$$-6\ 1$$
$$-7\ 2.$$

There had to be a clue somewhere. I read aloud the first row of unchanging numbers: one, two, seven. One to seven! That could be the clue; each color was represented by a number from one through seven. But how could I determine those numbers? The rainbow on the display gave me a possible answer. Seven colors and seven numbers in order from the red on the outside curve of the rainbow to violet on the inside curve. If I was right, then red equaled one, orange equaled two, yellow equaled three, green equaled four, blue equaled five, indigo equaled six, and violet equaled seven.

Whatever the equation was, the solution had to be a number more than zero and less than eight if I was right. I was trying to figure out the equation when a stocky man with close-cut gray hair came through the door. He quickly fell flat on the floor and spread out his arms and legs to minimize the danger of the holes. He looked at me and, pointing to the dead woman, asked, "What is she to you?"

"A stranger. I think she's dead. I've almost figured out the equation that determines which tiles collapse next. Do you know it?"

He said, "No," as he crawled to the woman, avoiding the holes in a practiced way that showed he was familiar with the tiles. When he reached the woman's side, he lifted her right wrist with his left hand. I thought he was checking for a pulse until his right hand came out of his waist pouch with a knife.

I watched in horror as he pressed his knife against her wrist just below an emerald green bracelet she wore. I turned away as he began a sawing motion with the knife. I pressed my hands against my ears to block out the screech as the knife cut through bone and gristle.

When the noise stopped, I looked at him as he removed the green bracelet from her severed wrist. He put both bracelet and knife back in his waist pouch. I saw that he wore a gray bracelet of the same kind on his right wrist.

There was no longer room for me to stand on the ledge. The moving wall was pushing me onto the tiles. I jumped down to my knees, avoiding the open holes. Then I quickly imitated the stranger's spread eagle position, carefully avoiding the holes and slowly moving toward the door. The stranger said, "Move quickly, blanc, if you're going to get out before the drains open."

I looked at the display and read the numbers:

$$1\ 2\ 7$$
$$-6\ 2$$
$$-5\ 2.$$

As fast as I could think I tried finding an equation that would give me answers from one through seven. On the third try I got one that worked. The first number in the first row was multiplied by the first number of a pair. The second number in the first row was the power to which the second number of the pair was raised. The third number was added to the sum of the first two calculations.

I mentally plugged the numbers into the equation and got the answers, six and five which meant the colors indigo and blue. I looked around and saw that the indigo and blue tiles had collapsed. I'd done it. I'd figured it out!

As I moved toward the door, the display changed to read:

$$1\ 2\ 7$$
$$-6\ 1$$
$$-7\ 2.$$

I solved the equation twice and got the answers orange and green. I got up from my prone position and began running toward the door. The stranger was ahead of me. I shouted, "The orange and green tiles are going to disappear. Watch out!"

By the time the orange and green tiles had collapsed, the stranger and I both made it through the door.

He looked at me in awe, saying, "You did it! You figured it out."

The door shut. I looked around. To the right was an open portal marked by a circle around a rainbow. That must be the winner's circle that the woman told me about. I started toward it.

The stranger grabbed me by the wrist and said, "Don't go in there or you'll be punished. The winner's circle is for players with wristlocks, not blancs."

He pointed to the gray bracelet on his wrist. "Where's yours?"

My right wrist was naked. I shook my head. "If I'm not a player, what am I?"

"You're a blanc. Do you remember anything that happened before you found yourself in the room with the colored tiles?"

"No. Nothing, nothing at all. Do you know me? Do you know my name?"

He shook his head no. "If you need a name, why don't you call yourself Rathe?"

I tried the name by saying it aloud. It sounded all right but what name wouldn't to a person with no past and no memory. "Thanks, I'll be Rathe. What's your name?"

"Errox."

It was completely unfamiliar. "If I can't go to the winner's circle, where do I go?"

Errox said, "Follow me, if you want to get out of here alive."

I followed him to the left into a small passageway that sloped down. I pondered just what he'd meant by his comment about getting out alive—we had already survived the room of collapsing tiles. What other dangers were there inside this labyrinth.

Errox's manner was brusque and didn't invite questions. We walked through the passageway, made another turn until we reached a solid wall with a metal panel. Errox bent down and opened the access panel, pushing it to the side. He stooped down and entered, while I followed. We emerged in a room full of spheroid machinery.

"Errox, I need your help! I can't remember anything. I don't know who I am or where we are."

He motioned for me to be quiet. I listened hard and heard a faint noise coming through the walls. It sounded like the distant murmur of conversation but I couldn't make out any words. Errox appeared to know where he was going and led me to another access panel. He opened it, using his still bloody knife, and we entered a room with a wide sloping chute at one end. I heard the sound of running water.

"Get ready to swim," he said. Water poured into the room. Soon it was up to my waist. Something jostled me—a dead body! It wasn't the dead woman I'd watched die in the first room. The body was male, its mouth and eyes wide-open; it looked like the personification of death. The hair on the back of my neck rose and my skin prickled. Errox studied the body. When he removed the knife from his waist pouch I turned my head so I wouldn't have to watch him mutilate another corpse for its wristband.

Errox cursed loudly as he wrestled with the body in the water that had now become level with my chest. He was having trouble severing the corpse's wrist. He took hold of the hand and ripped it off the partially severed wrist. As soon as he removed the band

and let go of the mutilated corpse, it quickly swirled away in the rising water.

I saw other bodies and body parts floating into the chamber. The water level kept rising. Now it was up to my shoulders. Errox was no longer trying to salvage the colored wristbands from corpses. He was bobbing up and down in the water.

The water level rose and swept me off my feet. I tried to regain my footing and failed. I didn't know how to swim!

My mouth filled with water and I sank like a stone.

Choking and sputtering, I fought my way to the surface. Something bumped me and I opened my eyes; I was face-to-face with the body of the woman who died in the first room! I tried to scream and swallowed more water in the attempt. I went under again with my heart beating like a drum. My lungs cried out for air. I was drowning!

Something or someone grabbed my tunic at the back of my head and pulled me to the surface. I gulped huge mouthfuls of air, coughing and sputtering as I bobbed up and down in the water. Only Errox's firm grip kept me from drowning.

"Take a deep breath."

I filled my burning lungs with air just as the wall at the narrow end of the room swung up out of sight. I felt the swift current as the water flowed toward the opening. Just as I started to go under again, I heard Errox cry out. "Don't fight it!"

I closed my eyes to keep out the water and something slammed hard into my face, loosening my teeth and turning everything into a whirling black vortex.

TWO

I came to coughing and sputtering. I felt a hand lift me out of the water. My gradual return to consciousness was accompanied by a burning soreness in my throat and a throbbing pain in my left hip. Someone was pounding me on the back and shoulders.

"Breathe, damn you! Get up!"

Nausea shook my stomach as I stumbled to my feet. Errox stopped thumping my back and pushed me toward a small stream of water running in the center of a wide channel. I would have drowned if he hadn't helped me. I fell to my knees and felt the hard pressure in my stomach erupt through my throat and out my mouth. The stream carried the vomit away.

When the spasms stopped, I cleaned my face and mouth with the fresh smelling water. I only drank several mouthfuls, but something warned me against quickly filling my stomach. It was obvious I knew *things*; what I didn't know was my identity or where I was now.

I tried to organize my thoughts, but my memory was like an almost empty bottle holding only the recent horrors. I turned away from the stream and saw the oval face of Errox with high cheekbones, yellowish skin and eyes like black pools, so dark that there appeared to be no separation between pupil and iris.

"Thank you, Errox! You saved my life."

Errox eyed me like a diner examining an unidentified morsel, not sure that it was worth eating. "What do you remember?"

"I don't remember anything before waking up in the room with the colored tiles. Can you tell me anything? Who I am or why I was there?"

"No." His voice was steady and hard, like his limbs.

"What is that place called?"

"It's the Rainbow Run."

"What is its purpose?"

He shook his head. "We don't have time for questions now. Keep quiet, and follow me." His manner was stern and decisive with a hint of menace.

The confidence that breaking the color codes had given me had been eroded by the rushing water that almost drowned me and now by Errox's bluntness. I followed him meekly as he led me down the channel to a spot where the wall was lowest. He went over it in a single, smooth leap. I scrambled after him, shivering in my wet tunic. We climbed up a grassy bank. I looked around; the horizon was dominated by a nearby mesa of gray buildings without obvious doors or windows. The megalithic structures covered both sides of the bank as far as I could see in either direction.

Although my legs were longer than Errox's stout limbs, I had to walk quickly to match his brisk stride. As we neared the buildings, there was a loud hum that I heard and felt. I pressed my hand against the wall of the first building we reached and felt my bones vibrate.

There were no people. Every thousand paces or so there were narrow corridors which revealed only more mountainous structures. I lingered briefly near a hot air vent.

While I was trying to dry my still wet tunic, Errox turned into a corridor and vanished from my sight. My heart hammered as I hurried to catch up; I needed my guide despite whatever reservations I had about his behavior inside the Rainbow Room and his indifference to my plight. I turned the corner and saw Errox ahead, motioning impatiently for me to hurry. By the time I caught up with him I was winded. He waited for me to catch my breath. Then he led me down a narrow passageway.

I needed all my concentration to keep my weary legs moving. It seemed like an eternity passed before he stopped to let me rest. He didn't appear to be the least bit tired. I gave him a thankful nod and leaned against a wall.

"We'll be through the autofactory sector soon," Errox said.

Questions filled my mind but I was unwilling to ask them because I was dead tired and unsure whether I would get meaningful answers—or any answers at all. Why had Errox been in the color room? Why had he wanted the dead woman's green wristlock? Did he have some ulterior motive in saving me from drowning?

We made two more rest stops before reaching the end of the corridor where there was a large slideway with ten slidestrips moving in each direction. The slow moving slidestrips were on the outside.

As we stepped onto one of the slow-moving slidestrips—a motion my body made automatically as though from long practice—Errox said, "Walk beside me and stay on the same slidestrip. Keep your right hand in the folds of your tunic so no one can see that you aren't wearing a wristlock. If anyone speaks to us, I'll answer."

I noticed that everyone we passed wore a wristlock on their right hand. They were of many hues, although the majority were gray. I stayed alert for the first dozen blocks, expecting to be challenged at any time. The people I saw were a variety of shapes and colors but all wore the plain brown tunics. All of them wore colored wristlocks. No one even noticed me. I avoided direct eye contact but scanned every face looking for someone, something, anything familiar. I didn't find it. I was lost in a world of strangers.

We passed huge pyramidal structures, built with steep, receding blocks, separated from each other by wide walkways. I had to crane my neck to see the peaks. The pyramids were different colors, like the slidestrips, with one wide portal on the bottom floor. All the windows were opaque and I wondered if they were made from one-way glass to conceal peering faces.

Several times we took slideway exits to elevated cross slidestrips. I lost all sense of direction. Errox seemed to be following a remembered route because there were no directional markers that I could discern. As we approached one of the pyramids, Errox guided me off the slidestrip and onto the gray building's front lip. Errox said, "We're going into this urbode. Stay close and follow me."

Errox nodded a greeting to a gaunt man wearing a gray wristlock who appeared to be guarding the portal. The guard acknowledged the nod. Errox placed his wristlock against the portal's silver plate and the door opened. I followed Errox as closely if I were his shadow.

The entrance hall was jammed with people of both sexes and various colors, white, yellow, black and various shades of brown. Many of the people nodded to Errox while others seemed to ignore his passage. I stayed as close to him as possible, sensing an undercurrent of potential hostility that seemed to be directed toward Errox or me, or maybe both of us.

At the main elevator bank, Errox used his wristlock to open the doors. We went up to the fifteenth floor and got off. The walls and floors were surprisingly immaculate considering the large number of residents, some of whom obviously lacked the cleanliness habit.

Everything seemed new to me. Nothing stirred any memory of a past before the Rainbow Room. My brief conversations with the woman who died and with Errox assured me that I knew the language, but I knew nothing of how these people lived or survived in this culture.

Errox stopped in front of a door with three embossed diamonds over two crescents. He pressed his wristlock against the doorplate and we passed through an anteroom into the common room, where five people sat on furniture built into the wall. Three of them started talking to Errox at once.

Errox held up his hand and the talking ceased. Turning to a tall, thin man with a bony face, he said, "Geeter, this is Rathe. Take him to the sleep room."

To me, he said, "Go with Geeter."

I followed Geeter through another room, past an archway, and down a long hall. Geeter stopped and pressed his wristlock against the doorplate of the fourth doorway. As soon as the door opened, he motioned for me to enter, saying, "Sleep well and may you find your rainbow in your dreams."

"Thanks, Geeter," I replied, pleased to know the name of one more person in this world of strangers.

I lowered my exhausted body onto a raised sleeping platform. As the bed cushion conformed to my body shape, I began to mentally playback the day's events. They made no more sense to me upon reflection than they had when they were occurring. I slowly drifted into sleep, hoping that my subconscious would dredge up clues as to my identity, my past—and to my present predicament.

*   *   *

I awoke with a dry mouth and a full bladder. I stumbled through an archway to the sleeproom lav. After urinating and drinking from the bubbler, I tried to recall my dreams. All I remembered were confused images of multicolored tiles disappearing as I tried to walk on them and being swept away by a river's current, carried down a channel toward an unknown destination.

I cleaned my hands with the ultrasonic washer and peered into the mirror. The lean face peering back was neither familiar nor unfamiliar. The nose appeared too large for my thin face. My skin, prison pallor gray, was stretched tightly over the bones of my face. My brown hair, like that of all the other men I'd seen, was cut short in stubble.

The only surprise was my eyes; they seemed to burn with their own inner light. I remembered a phrase—"the rich gleam of fanaticism"—which seemed to describe my eyes. Where the phrase came from, I did not know. No other memories were forthcoming. Looking into my blue eyes, wondering what they had seen, made me uncomfortable with my own staring.

The rumbling of my stomach reminded me that I was hungry. I had no memory of eating before or after I came to in the Rainbow Room. I went to the door intending to go out and search for food, but the door wouldn't open. I remembered Errox using his wristlock to open doors. My wrist looked very bare.

I was trapped, a captive of Errox's unknown intentions. I started shivering and my heart began to pound. I hit the door with my fists, trying to attract someone, anyone's attention. Either no one heard me or I was being ignored. As my heartbeat slowed, I realized that I didn't want these strangers to think that I had panicked. I fell back on the bed and endeavored to keep despair at bay.

Sometime later, a lean, tense woman with sharp features opened the door and said, "Hello, my name is Ural."

"I'm Rathe."

"I know. Would you like something to eat?"

"I'm famished." I couldn't remember the last time I ate.

I followed Ural into a room where six people, including Geeter, were sitting on the floor and eating. All of them wore gray wristlocks. Ural said, "Sit down and I'll bring food."

She brought a crystal flask of amber liquid and a translucent pale blue plate laden with rose, aqua and violet cubes. I automatically bit off the top of the flask and ate it, then drank deeply of the warm, satisfying fluid. I was surprised by my automatic reactions—my reflexes were in better shape than my memory. I must have known the flask was eatable, which proved I'd eaten them before. I believed that was important information; it meant that I was lost, but not a stranger to this world.

The food cubes were excellent, but when I'd finished them I was still hungry. When I saw the others eating their plates I started taking bites of my own plate, which was crispy but with a surprisingly sweet taste.

After finishing the plate, I sipped from the flask and studied the others. Most of them were unkempt except for a big-boned man who reminded me of Errox. Geeter looked at me. I asked him, "Is this your first meal?"

"Yeah. How was your sleep?"

"The best I can remember."

Geeter wheezed several times and said, "Nothing like a sense of humor."

Geeter turned away when the big-boned man gave him a stern look. I felt uncomfortable but I had no place to go and no wristlock to open doors. I didn't like the feeling I had of being at their mercy, since these people didn't appear to be very caring.

I sat quietly and sipped my drink. A small man with a finely sculpted face entered the room looking out of place compared to the rest of the grays in the room. His tunic was clean and he had a confident air about him that most of the grays I'd met lacked.

The newcomer asked, "Where is the new blanc?"

Ural pointed to me. The small man sat beside me and said, "I'm Kahalyton."

"I'm Rathe," I replied.

Kahalyton's brown eyes brightened. "You remember your name?"

"No. Errox gave me my name."

"Do you remember anything about your former life, anything at all?"

"No," I answered. "I know the language and the names of common objects, but I can't remember anything that happened before I came here." Saying that out loud brought an incoming tide of black despair that threatened to engulf me.

Kahalyton's hands gripped my shoulders with a surprising firmness. "You're not the only one, Rathe. Dozens of blancs appear here in Azrath daily. No one knows where they come from or why they are here. Some think that Kara has forsaken the House of Rebirth, although the intermediaries deny that."

"You mean there are others like me?"

"Yes, but we don't see very many of them. Most get taken into custody by the VIS and are taken to an imprinting center."

"Who are the VIS?"

"The Variation Investigation Service; they try to preserve the status quo."

"What does the imprinting do?"

"It's supposed to provide blancs with a new personal history. In practice, the blancs get the bare minimum of information necessary for survival. Most of them end up as perms, like the people in this urbode." He pointed to his wristlock.

It was gray.

His eyes followed mine and he smiled. "I'm a gray by choice, not like these—" He stopped when the big-boned gray glared at him. "Anyway, you are not alone."

I felt somewhat better knowing that I was not the only one dumped into a strange, dangerous place with no memory.

Kahalyton asked, "Where were you when you regained consciousness?"

"In a place that Errox called the Rainbow Room."

"How did you survive and find your way here?"

"Errox helped me escape that room and brought me to this urbode."

Kahalyton seemed surprised and asked, "Errox was in the Rainbow Room?"

"Yes. What is the purpose of that place?" I asked.

"It is a place where anyone can take a chance to raise their color level without playing the Game. It's very dangerous, as you probably noticed. Do you know what the wristlocks are for?"

"All I know is that they open doors and that they come in different colors. Nothing else."

"In this world the wristlock is the key to life, at least in the cities. It's different in the countryside. But here: what you can do; where you can go; how long you can stay; even how long you live—all of these are determined by the color of your wristlock. The magic key to freedom is the rainbow wristlock. All doors are open to the rainbow, including the portal of eternal life."

"What determines the color of one's wristlock?"

"How well they play the Game, which is the steady route to advancement. The Game challenges the intelligence, judgment, intuition, creativity, senses, and all the more subtle characteristics of the mind. If you have the intelligence and are willing to spend half a season playing the Game, you can raise one color level. There are thirty-six colors on the rainbow road; few players ever rise above saffron, the twentieth level."

"How does the Rainbow Room fit into the Game?"

"The Rainbow Room is part of an alternative, a very dangerous alternative known as the Color Wheel, to the Game. It is for death-defying players. People who enter the Color Wheel risk their lives in hopes of advancing through the colors without playing the Game in the ordinary way. There is a choice of environments—the Mirror Maze, the Vibration Vessel, the Laser Lobby, the Hunting House, the Bouncing Ballroom, and the Rainbow Room. Some enter hoping for a better life; others enter seeking the certainty of death."

I had been dumped in the Rainbow Room to die. There was no other explanation. I didn't know why it was done to me, but I was going to find out why. When I did, I would punish whoever was responsible. To do that I needed a lot more information about the world I found myself abandoned in.

"Have you ever been inside the Color Wheel?" I asked.

"No, Rathe. I like to think that I'm too smart to play such a longshot. I played the Game well. In less than twenty seasons I rose to magenta, the thirty-second level. And there I was stuck—four levels below eternal life, unable to advance no matter how diligently I played the Game. I knew rainbows that were less intelligent, less astute, less perceptive, less skilled...

"I began to question everything. I took a critical look around me and I didn't like what I saw. My friends and contemporaries were slaves to the Game; it demanded their complete attention—it devoured their lives! It struck me that playing the Game was slavery; the higher the hue, the tighter the chains."

Kahalyton's voice grew louder as he remembered his failings. He was making the other occupants of the room uncomfortable. Two of them got up and left; the one woman who was still crunching on her plate ignored us.

Kahalyton continued talking. "So I stopped playing. My former friends dropped away like leaves in winter as the color of my wristlock degraded. It takes a long time for a magenta wristlock to turn gray—a very long time. During that period I learned a lot about myself and about this society. I learned that the color of a wristlock does not determine a person's worth. I learned that—"

Kahalyton stopped speaking when Errox entered the room. When Errox glared at him, he jumped up and said, "Excuse me, Rathe, but I have to go. I'll talk with you later."

Errox watched Kahalyton's exit with a predatory grin as if pleased by the anxiety he had created with his entrance.

Ural said, "So he thinks he's the one who'll save us. That's a laugh."

She and Errox laughed in a way that had little to do with amusement.

Errox put his hand on my shoulder. I jumped it was so unexpected.

"How are they treating you?" he asked.

"Fine," I answered, too quickly to sound convincing. A couple of the grays quickly looked away.

Errox frowned and said, "If anyone bothers you, tell me. I'll take care of them."

"What about a wristlock? I can't leave the building without one."

"It'll take time. Until then enjoy yourself. Leave the worrying to me." He turned and pointed at a washed-out looking woman with a gray wristlock, he grinned lewdly and said, "Anything you want here is yours."

That brought me a hostile look from the big boned gray man. Why was Errox so friendly to me and not to the others? All of them, even the big gray, seemed afraid of him. What power did he have? Why did the others stay if they were scared?

"Remember Rathe, it's not safe to leave the urbode without a wristlock and a reliable guide. If you don't have both, the VIS will get you. If that happens, even I won't be able to save you."

THREE

I was back in the sleeproom, but sleep was not forthcoming, nor were any of my former memories. I'd spent the previous evening alone in this small cubicle in Ural's dwell, thinking about what Kahalyton had told me the day before. I tried to find some pattern based on what little I knew; all I found were more questions and no answers.

Other than Errox, Kahalyton was the only person who had shown any interest in me. The other grays acted as if I were invisible. Kahalyton told me that this dwell belonged to Ural. I wondered how or why someone like Ural came to possess such a large residence. She refused to answer my questions about that or anything else.

From the abrupt way Ural treated me, even I could see she only tolerated me because Errox told her to. Why was she so afraid of him?

Errox was in a dominant position with me because I knew nothing, but his hold over Ural was different, not only in degree but in kind. The other grays deferred to Ural, but not to the extent they kowtowed to Errox. From a conversation I'd overheard I knew that everyone would be leaving Ural's dwell soon. I didn't know why and I didn't ask because I knew I would be rebuffed again. There was an obvious undercurrent of dislike aimed at me. Was it because Errox had picked me for some role or action in one of his schemes and the other grays were jealous? I didn't know enough about him, or them, to put it together.

My sleeproom was unlocked, unlike the one I'd spent my first night in. Perhaps someone—maybe Ural, maybe Errox—believed I could be trusted now. But trusted for what was the nagging question. It was too complex a question for me to answer; I didn't even have answers to simple questions, such as what was my real name?

I didn't know whether the grays crowded together in Ural's quarters because of necessity or for companionship. If it was for companionship, I knew it wasn't for mine. Most of them ignored me unless they were following Errox's orders to take care of me while he was gone.

After using the lav, I examined myself in the mirror while cleaning my hands. I practiced smiling with grim results: my thin lips spread flat against slightly irregular teeth, displaying a narrow crescent beneath a long nose. The smile didn't extend to my icy gaze. I looked as if I were trying to frighten someone by appearing sinister.

I ran my hands forward over my bristly hair before leaving the lav and going to the kitchen. No one was there so I couldn't ask about the eating schedule. I went to a room Geeter had called the gameroom; it was also empty. That was fine with me. I didn't want to force myself on the grays who looked through me as if I were not there. Did they think my amnesia was catching? Why was there so much prejudice directed toward blancs? Or was it just me?

I sat down in one of the low-slung chairs to rest, weary of trying to make sense of my limited store of information. The chair adapted itself to my body contours. I tried to relax, wishing I could let my mind drift among pleasant memories, but all of my memories were recent and most of them were negative or, at best, neutral.

My hands rested on some controls that were built into the chair arms. Suddenly I knew with certainty that these were game controls, the devices used to play the Game. I knew what they were! Was my memory beginning to return?

The controls were familiar to my hands but new to my conscious mind. My fingers began to rotate the gyroscopic spheres with a dexterity that would have been surprising if it hadn't felt so ordinary.

Five multicolored holographic patterns appeared in the center of the room like images summoned from another dimension. I watched the kaleidoscopic changes, delighted to have something to engage my restless mind. My fingers moved over the smooth controls in a process as automatic as removing beard bristles from my face. My capable hands merged the elements of the first image into a pattern that seemed familiar.

Fascinated, I watched a greenish blue mandala of interlocking complexity reveal its delicate detail—azure circles around aqua hexagrams and deep green triangles nested in bright blue spheres. All the details of the mandala slowly turned for five complete revolutions and then the pattern stabilized, indicating I had mastered the first level of this part of the Game.

I had stabilized the first holo pattern. *I can do it! I have power and competence. I can play the Game and achieve. Perhaps I do belong in this world.*

Eagerly I went to work on the second holo pattern. It was a blur of orange, red, and gold. My educated fingers led the outer shape into a geodesic dome made of translucent golden triangles. It felt right. I went to work manipulating the inner construction again and again until I perceived a three-dimensional maze of orange flames. Deep in the heart of the flames, at the center of the maze, I saw small bright red spheres in Brownian motion. With semi-automatic movement of the controls, I separated one red sphere from the rest and ran it through the maze. I placed it at an intersection of the triangles.

It stayed!

I picked out another red ball and began to repeat the procedure, going through another section of the maze. I was able to visualize what should happen next. I had a mental picture of the complete holopattern and understood the clues it would give me about the third pattern.

I watched the balls run and knew that I could run through the rest of the patterns. I was not as helpless as I had thought. Maybe I could become a rainbow. But first I would need my own wristlock. Was it possible I had been a rainbow before I was dropped into the Rainbow Room?

"What are you doing to me?!!" Ural screamed, as she jerked the controls out of my hands and stuffed them back into the chair. She and three anonymous grays, who I hadn't seen come in, were all looking at me with naked hostility.

The holopatterns winked out of existence.

Surprised and confused, I angrily asked, "Why did you do that? I could have stabilized all five patterns."

"Oh, wonderful! Had you completed that last set, I would have found myself eligible for a red wristlock. I've been a gray for more than twenty seasons—and I *never* play the Game. The VIS would have brought me in for questioning before the third meal, never to return."

"Ural, you could tell them I did it."

"You don't own a wristlock!" she cried. "You're a blanc, a non-person. YOU HAVE NO IDENTITY! If they believed me, I'd face correction for not reporting your existence to a nu-blanc reporting center. Damn Errox and his blasted schemes! I told him it was dangerous to move you from that locked room. I curse the day I ever agreed to take you in."

Two of the three grays appeared agitated during Ural's outburst, while the third one eyed me warily. Was this because I had upset Ural, or because I played the Game so well? I didn't know but I knew enough not to ask.

Ural looked me straight in the face as if her pale blue eyes were drills that could penetrate my skull. In a barely controlled voice, she said, "Some of the people here are loyal to *me.* If you ever touch these controls again I'll have them break your arms and then toss you onto the slideway. If you do anything to bring the VIS around, I'll have you tossed off it—Errox or no Errox."

I couldn't think of a safe reply. There were currents and riptides all around me, but I had no sense of direction. Nor was there a safe harbor. I'd been cast adrift in a world of mystery. Until

I learned to navigate it better, I would have to float along on the surface and be wary of every current and undertow.

I sat in silence until a fat man came in and said, "Time to eat."

I joined the grays in the dining area. I ate my servings in silence. The conversations around me were bland and superficial, too dull to be contrivances designed to shut me out.

When I finished eating I went to the sleeproom and got into bed. My head was full of questions: What were Errox's plans for me? How would Errox react when Ural told him about how she caught me playing the Game? Just who were the Variation Investigation Service and what rules did they enforce? Would I ever get a chance to pursue a rainbow wristlock of my own?

Later I heard a babble of voices greeting Errox. I left the sleeproom just in time to see Ural whispering intently to his ear. He brushed the others aside and followed Ural into her sleeproom. The door slammed behind them.

My concern about Errox's reaction intensified. I went into the empty dining area and paced back and forth. I didn't have enough data to predict Errox's reaction to my playing the Game.

My mental stage became crowded with unbidden images—the one that wouldn't go away was of Errox cutting off the wrist of the woman in the Rainbow Room. I wondered if that was a harbinger of things to come.

The images vanished as Errox came into the room. He looked around to make certain we were alone and said, "Rathe, I've got good news for you. I've made arrangements to get you a wristlock."

"That's great," I said, hiding my concern and wondering what kind of favor Errox would ask of me in return.

"After you get your own wristlock, I'll take you to another dwell where no one will know you were a blanc."

I felt relief tinged with wariness. I also knew this wasn't the time to ask questions. I said, "That is very good news, Errox."

He smiled as if he had some secret knowledge and said, "Wait here."

I waited for what seemed a long time. I was feeling anxious by the time he returned. He came in, jerked his thumb to indicate I should go with him. I followed him wordlessly, out of Ural's dwell, out of the building and onto a series of slidestrips, keeping my naked right wrist concealed in the folds of my tunic. Our route took us through the grid of multi-hued pyramids with their windows as opaque as my past. If my situation weren't so precarious, it might have been a holiday outing.

Feeling more confident now that I was about to get a wristlock and a different dwell, I attempted to talk with Errox, being careful not to ask questions, but leaving openings for volunteered information. "Your knowledge of this area is impressive. I've lost track of all the directional changes and couldn't find my way to Ural's dwell without help."

"You will pick up navigational ability once you have a wristlock and can move around freely."

"The only landmarks I've seen are the Color Wheel and the autofactory sector. Other than their different colors, all these urbodes seem identical on the outside."

"Yes." he replied. "That's why some of the permanent grays function as runners, spotters, and messengers. Some have fantastic memory systems and others used knotted strips of old tunics as memory aids. A fortunate few like me have an inner location sense and always know where they are."

I suspected that this ability was one of the reasons the other grays deferred to Errox. "Wouldn't it be simpler to identify all the structures and slidestrips?" I asked, and then realized that I'd done a no-no—asked a question.

"The VIS label any attempt to post directions a defacing offense." Errox said in a forbidding tone that ended the conversation.

I wondered what the VIS agents thought about the scratched symbols I saw on Ural's door. Or were they too insignificant to be an offense? I hated that I knew so little about this world and my own past.

I followed Errox's lead as he moved from one slidestrip to another. Previously, I'd thought the many changes of direction might be to keep me dependent on Errox for orientation. Now I knew that Errox followed some inner compass that I would never know. Was I doomed to be a lost soul in this world of multi-colored pyramids for the rest of my days? No, I'd find my way. If the grays in Ural's dwell could find their way around, certainly someone like myself who appeared able to master the Game should find it possible.

I wondered why directional signs and markings were forbidden. What purpose could such prohibitions serve? I was certain that the answer to that question was critical to my making any sense of this world. Once I had my wristlock and my new dwell, I would try to learn my own routes, work toward traveling independently, and start digging for the answers to the hundreds of questions that filled my waking mind to the bursting point.

Errox motioned for me to follow him as he moved to the right to the slowest strip. I kept my bare wrist hidden in the fullness of my tunic, not knowing where the VIS were but aware that people were expected to report all blanc sightings. We moved from the slowest slidestrip onto the walkway in front of a row of urbodes.

I suspected that Errox was counting to himself in order to find a particular urbode but I saw no sign of it on his face. His lips didn't move and his eyes gave nothing away. He stopped before the portal of one of the identical looking gray urbodes and I realized that we had reached our destination.

A stocky woman stood guard at the entrance. With monotonous regularity she raised herself up on her toes and then lowered herself down on her heels. She did it as if it were a ritual or an old habit. Below her tunic, her bulging calf muscles were as big around as my thighs. All of her muscles that I could see looked as hard as Errox's eyes. There were also the usual gray spotters and knot weavers that seemed to be a constant before every urbode. She stared at Errox with a challenging expression.

He said one word to her. It sounded like "Hushel" to me. I had no memory of ever having heard the word before; I didn't know whether it was a name or a code word. But whatever it was, it was the right word. The tough looking woman moved aside to let Errox press his wristlock against the door plate.

The door opened. I crowded in closely behind him, eager to be off the walkway. We passed the elevator banks and continued down the corridor to the fifth cross passage. We turned right and passed eleven doorways, when we reached the twelfth, Errox said, "Wait here until I come back."

Errox entered a door a few steps away. As that door closed, I saw another one farther down the hallway open. A woman stepped out of the opened door and into the corridor. She was tall, almost my height, and slim. She stared at me with a provocative intensity.

Unlike everyone else I'd met, she was looking at my face, not at the naked wrist I kept concealed. She drew nearer, still examining my face. In a throaty whisper she asked, "Vargan, is it you?"

"I don't know...?"

"It is you. I could feel your presence in the building. You didn't know that would be one of the side effects, did you?"

"I've lost my memory. I don't remember you and I don't know what you're talking about. You know me?"

"Come closer." I moved toward her. She looked deep into my eyes. "Yes, it's you. What's this about your memory? Is this some new game you've devised to taunt me?"

"I'm not playing any game with you. My memory's gone."

"You've changed...I knew they would catch you sooner or later because you're a danger to them. You're thinner too and look like you've suffered. But you haven't suffered as much as I have."

"Are you sure you know me?"

She smiled and said, "Of course. I'd know you in the dark at a love feast." She took me by the hand to lead me through the open door and into her abode. "Come in. Come with me, Vargan. I will help you remember. I haven't forgotten a single thing that you taught me."

Fascinated, I followed obediently.

FOUR

"I want the door to stay open," I said, "I need to see the corridor."

"That's the Vargan I know, always one eye looking for an opportunity. Put your foot forward on that button and it will keep the door open."

I shifted positions so I could watch the door that Errox had entered. That was where I'd get my wristlock. Then Errox would take me to different dwell, one where I wouldn't be known as a blanc.

She pressed her body against mine as if magnetized, molding herself against me like a second skin. Her warmth was comforting, her ardor disconcerting and appealing at the same time. She was attractive and willing. Her breasts were spherical and firm; I could feel them pressing against my ribs. If it wasn't my imagination, her nipples were hard.

Keeping my foot on the door cell in the floor, I put my arms around her. I couldn't remember the last time I had sexual relations. I had no memory of sexual experiences but I could recall the sensations. I felt sure I would know what to do and how to do it, but now wasn't the time. She writhed against me as if possessed by an all-consuming passion, saying Vargan over and over in an erotic incantation that sent waves of desire through my flesh.

I was lost in her seductive wiles. She had me enveloped in her sensuality and sounds. Was I Vargan? The name grew more familiar with her continuing repetition, but had it been familiar when I first heard it? I couldn't remember....

With both hands I moved her upper body so I could look into her face. I asked, "What's your name?"

Her eyes snapped open. She asked, "You don't remember? After all the things you've done to me, you don't remember my name!"

She stopped grinding her pelvis against me. My eyes were trapped by her gaze. She had strange-looking light brown eyes, eyes that looked like gray stones with a translucent brown overlay.

"I'm sorry. I don't remember anything about me either, not my name or anything else."

"Your name is Vargan and you're a riplocker. I don't love you, but I must have you as a lover. You possess me, now and forever. We are bound together by more than the ties of our lust."

"Please tell me your name."

"Lyonella. Look me in the eye and tell me that you never heard my name before, that you don't remember the time of sexual enchantment, our time of intoxication and decadence."

I stared intently into her face. Her eyebrows were perfect arcs above large eyes that slightly protruded from heavy lids. Her eyes appeared out of focus and I noticed an intensity that didn't appear normal.

"I have no memory of ever saying or hearing the name Lyonella before you just spoke it. Nor do I have any memory of being Vargan. I want you to believe me. I need your help to learn about myself and who I am. Please?"

"I see you still have the ability to tell the boldest lie while appearing sincere, but you forget who I am. I am a woman for all cycles, not a perm-gray voluptuary fresh out of the House of Rebirth suffering from transit fugue."

"This is no game. I don't know who I am. I don't know you. Why won't you believe me?"

"Because you were watching the entrance of the dwell of Hushel, the wristlock smitty, and because you're not wearing your wristlock. Who are you hiding from?"

Lyonella's statements confirmed that Hushel dealt in wristlocks. I looked at her wrist again and realized that she was the first person I'd talked to who wasn't a gray. She was different from them. Was that difference caused by her knowledge of me or was it that she was delusional or crazy?

"It's true I'm here for a wristlock. I don't deny that, but I was brought here. I don't know any more about where I am than I know who I am."

"Can you deny the flesh, Vargan?"

Before I could frame a response, Lyonella pressed her body against mine so strongly that I almost lost my balance. Her lips devoured my mouth. Her tongue explored the inside of my cheeks, my palate, my teeth, and strained to reach my uvula. Automatically I responded with an embrace that lasted until we both gasped.

As soon as she caught her breath, she said, "There has to be a way for us to be together. We can get away from this backwater.

I'm going to get better. The time between severe attacks is lengthening. We'll go someplace where they aren't organized enough to check immigrants. They won't have to know who you are and what you've done."

Every sentence she uttered made me more aware of how much I didn't know. I couldn't ask intelligent questions because I didn't understand the context. I didn't know what her problems were or even if they were connected to my unremembered past. The sexual desire I felt for her was warping my perspective. I had to keep focused on my first priority, getting a wristlock. I didn't know what to say to her. I could tell by the look on her face that she sensed my confusion. I wondered if I was so obvious that anyone could tell I was confused, or if she knew me well enough to be familiar with all my reactions.

"Your body responds to me," she said. "It always has. Why deny both of us? Take off your tunic and exercise those backwater tricks that seduced the sophisticate of Alura."

She stepped back from me, pulled off her tunic, and let it fall to the floor. I couldn't look away from her lean, shapely figure and the rich, brown triangle of pubic hair. She parted her thighs and said, "See. The scars are hardly noticeable. I bring you a beautiful body once again, the body that drove you to scar my mind."

I had a hard time taking in what she said; either I was a monster or she was mad. Had my memory been taken from me because I abused women? I made no move to accept her sexual offer, leery of what it might mean to her or me. Her voice became strident as she said, "So you reject me after closing me off from everything I ever had that wasn't you. I ought to notify the VIS."

I knew I didn't want that. "I can't stay with you now. I'm in this urbode to get a wristlock. After that I have to find my way to a new dwell. After I get relocated we can talk and I'll try to understand what you're telling me. I do want you and I want to know what you know about me. How can I find you again?"

"Find Hushel and I'll be nearby. You won't tell Hushel who I am, will you?" The bright glaze of paranoia crystallized in her eyes.

Hastily I promised, "I won't say anything about you to Hushel."

"How can I be sure? What am I to you but a damaged instrument of power? But I warn you...do not underestimate the extent of that power. I am still learning about it. Every time I survive the holocaust that you ignited in me, I become stronger."

Her presence disturbed me in multiple ways. Her voice and actions differed from what I'd seen and heard among the grays. When she bent over to pick up her tunic, the sight of the bare curves of her buttocks brought a lump to my throat. She snapped the tunic in the air and then began to tie fist-sized knots in it. I had no idea why she was doing that until she flicked it toward me, hitting the side of my head with the knotted end.

I gasped, lost my balance, and almost fell to the floor. She began screaming invectives at me in a loud voice, "Scum! Rake! Bum! Fake!" She repeated the words over and over as if chanting a curse while she continued slapping me with the tunic knots.

I moved into a defensive crouch, taking her blows on my arms. I managed to grab the tunic. With surprising strength, she jerked me off my feet. I panicked at the sound of the door closing. I let go of the tunic, lurched to my feet, and slammed my body into hers.

We fell in a tangled heap to the floor, our bodies in intimate, but hostile, contact. I was terrified at not being able to see Hushel's door, afraid I might not get a wristlock, half-afraid that I might not see my enigmatic guide again.

Lyonella's frenzied attack subsided, perhaps because my strength matched hers. She pressed her body against me as if trying to push me through the floor. When I braced myself, getting ready to heave her off me, her hand clutched my genitals. My body jerked in agony.

She twisted my sexual softness and the pain drove me berserk! I thrashed around like a madman, making spastic position changes. Using all my strength, I beat at her arms until she released me.

When she started rising up from the floor I hit the side of her head with a roundhouse blow that knocked her down. I rose and put my foot on the door cell. The door opened. As I limped into the corridor, she said, "It's all right, Vargan. You know this isn't the first time that you've beaten me."

I didn't like what she was implying, it felt wrong somehow. I had no memory of ever seeing her before, much less hitting her. I didn't bother to reply, because I was afraid I'd get caught up in her endless game of recriminations. I wasn't sure what kind of person I was before my memory fled, but I was almost certain that I wasn't anyone who beat women for pleasure or out of malice. I certainly hoped not....

The door closing behind me cut off her words. I straightened my tunic, ran my hand over my hair, while trying to calm the shakiness I felt after our violent, disturbing encounter. I was not quite composed when Hushel's door opened. Errox stepped out and looked toward the elevator where he had left me. When he turned and saw me in the corridor, he asked, "What are you doing down there?"

"Just pacing," I answered. I was surprised by how spontaneously the lie came out of my mouth, without a second thought. I didn't know whether or not I was Vargan, but Lyonella had said Vargan was an accomplished liar. As far as I knew it was the first lie I had ever told.

"Come in. Everything's ready." I saw Errox was now wearing a green wristlock; it brought back the image of Errox severing the wrist of the dead woman in the Rainbow Room. I shook my head to clear out the disturbing image and followed Errox into Hushel's quarters.

Errox introduced me to the wristlock smitty by saying, "Hushel, this is Rathe, the nu-blanc I told you about."

I wondered if Hushel would recognize me as Vargan. Lyonella knew him and he might have known me. From what Lyonella had said, I had surmised that wristlock smitty was an illegal pursuit. If so, Hushel was the kind of person Vargan would know.

Hushel, showing no sign of ever having seen me before, pointed to a chair and said, "Sit."

I wondered if he recognized me and was keeping quiet for reasons of his own, or because he didn't care who I was. I sat down in the chair, which had an unusual device built into the right arm. It was comprised of a strong metal frame around a short, hollow cylinder that ran along a track.

Hushel locked my right arm in the frame at the bend of my elbow. He attached fittings from five thick wires that ran through the cylinder to the ends of my fingers. Using a complex spreading tool, he carefully fitted a gray wristlock on the cylinder, treating the wristlock as if it were fragile.

I suspected that this was the gray wristlock that Errox had worn. Hushel touched a control on the frame and my fingers were pulled straight by the wires. He sprinkled a warm liquid over my hand that first tingled and then created numbness. He bound my numb hand and my wrist with a strip of silvery material. He pressed a lever on the frame and my hand was compressed to a degree I would have thought impossible.

When he turned a dial, the cylinder moved to cover my fingers and then my hand. For a moment it felt as if my hand was being crushed, then a sudden snap and the wristlock popped onto my wrist. Hushel disconnected me from the machine. I looked at the opaque grayness of the wristlock. I touched its smooth surface. I pulled at it and it stretched without appearing thinner.

"Don't do that!" Hushel shouted. "They only expand so far. If you pull it too hard, it'll blow your wrist off."

I gazed down at *my* wristlock. Had I been freer without it? I really had no way of knowing. With or without a wristlock, I was still more dependent on Errox than I wanted to be.

Hushel said, "Once the numbness wears off, your hand will be sore for several cycles. Don't see a medic about it. A medic would only notify the VIS. And, whatever you do, don't try to take it off yourself. There's an explosive charge in wristlocks that will shred your body into chunks the size of food cubes."

I stared down at my new wristlock with a newfound sense of fear and respect.

FIVE

After getting my wristlock I followed Errox out of the building. He said, "I'll take you to another urbode where you'll be able to stay. Don't tell anyone there or anywhere else that you were a blanc or how you got your wristlock."

I tried to make a map in my head of the slideway route we took but the many turns and reverses of direction made remembering difficult.

We arrived at a gray urbode no different from the rest, as far as I could discern. Errox led me inside and introduced me to Mirall, the pink-faced, blond-haired gray in charge of my new residence. He was slightly shorter than me and heavier. He seemed eager to please Errox and was friendly toward me. After Errox left, Mirall introduced me to some other resident grays. After glancing at my new wristlock, they seemed to accept me as one of their own. If they knew I'd been a blanc, they didn't care or mention it. Small talk and jarva juice seemed to be their major interests.

In my new dwell, I tried to rest and ignore the pain in my right hand. My thoughts turned to my missing memories, and then to Lyonella. The encounter with her made me wonder for the first time if I wanted to regain my memory. Was I Vargan, the shady, shadowy character whom Lyonella blamed for all her difficulties, or was this a case of mistaken identity? Could I merely be a stranger that she had coerced into her disjointed, troubled life?

I had mixed emotions about seeing Lyonella again. Even if I wanted to see her, I wouldn't know how to find her abode without assistance. I knew that I didn't want to ask Errox for help because I didn't want him to know I'd met her. I distrusted Errox. If he decided that he wanted her white wristlock, he wouldn't hesitate to harm Lyonella to obtain it—of that I was certain. Therefore, I must have known others like him in the past with his ruthless disregard for other people. If I had been like that myself, I didn't want to be that way any longer.

Regardless of whether or not I may have hurt Lyonella in the past, I didn't want to cause her any trouble now or in the future.

During the next two days I learned what I could about finding my way around. I was living in an urbode identical to the other ninety-nine urbodes that were in a large square bounded by slideways. On the other side of the slideways were other urbode complexes which from a distance appeared to be identical to the ones in this compound. From all viewpoints around the urbode, there appeared to be endless rows of urbodes as far as the eye could see. Wherever I was, I was just one unidentified mite among a teaming mass of humanity.

All the urbodes in the complex faced in the same direction, each with slidestrips heading toward a slideway that ran from left to right. From what I could find out, the grays in this complex found their way from one urbode to another by using a mental map. The first row of urbodes that faced the slidestrip was called front row one; the last row was called front row ten. The first line of urbodes on the left was called left line one; the last line, on the far right, was called left line ten. I lived in an urbode mentally identified as front row six/left line four.

With this map in my head I could find my way to any of the hundred urbodes in the square and get back again. I was pleased to have mastered even this small bit of orientation even though I had no one to visit in any of the other urbodes in the complex.

I was sitting alone, thinking about Lyonella and the possible implications of what she had said to me when Mirall interrupted my musing by saying, "Rathe, you have a visitor."

I knew it wasn't Errox because Mirall would have said his name. Could it be Lyonella? I felt both lust and apprehension about the possibility. I looked up as Mirall ushered Kahalyton into the room and left. I rose to greet him.

Kahalyton smiled and clasped both my hands in his. We exchanged nods and sat down. "You're a hard man to find, Rathe. I had to get some help to learn your whereabouts."

"Didn't Errox tell you where I am?"

"That one! We do not talk. I'm sure he would be displeased to find me here. Someday when I've drunk my fill of jarva, I will tell you all about him."

I didn't want to wait. I was desperate to know more about Errox, but not badly enough to risk driving my visitor away. After two days among Mirall's gray shadows, I craved significant conversation and stimulating companionship

"Why did you move?" Kahalyton asked.

"I felt uncomfortable at Ural's."

He nodded sagely. "Running into Ural's personality is like falling face down on a slidestrip. I can't see why Errox finds her attractive, but I'm certain they deserve each other."

I nodded in agreement.

"How are you getting along here, Rathe?"

"Better. At least I can come and go on my own," I said, proudly holding up my right arm to show my wristlock.

He started in surprise. "How did you come by that Rathe?"

"Errox arranged it."

Kahalyton grabbed my hand roughly and examined my wristlock. He made several clicking noises and said, "It doesn't look like a forgery. The VIS would put you through a cell-strip if they found a fake on you. Now I think I know why Errox was in the Rainbow Room, am I right?"

I shrugged my shoulders in feigned ignorance. Errox had told me not to tell anybody that I'd been a blanc or how I'd gotten a wristlock. Kahalyton already knew that I'd been a blanc and that Errox had brought me to Ural's. Maybe I'd already said too much, but Kahalyton was the only person who'd shown any interest in me, other than Lyonella. Still, I had only a limited amount of trust in Kahalyton.

"Errox told me not to tell anyone about the wristlock."

"For your sake, I hope this isn't one of his multiple-player scams."

"Multiple-player scam? What's that?"

"Sometimes two or more colors band together to help each other play the Game. If they are high hues, they sometimes get away with it—for a while."

The more I learned about this world, I found myself in, the less I cared for it.

"Why are the abodes so crowded?" I asked. "There are more grays here than at Ural's. Mirall has seventeen people here and a three-shift schedule for the sleep rooms."

"Ural has powerful associates. Most of the gray abodes are overcrowded. When I first slid down the color scale, a dwell like this would have housed six and been considered crowded if a seventh moved in. Things have changed rapidly. When I was a white just hitting my stride in the rainbow run, I talked to an elderly white who told me that only three or four grays shared a dwell when she had emerged from the House of Rebirth."

"Do all colors share dwells?"

"Almost all of the shades share dwells—the grays, beiges, blues, browns, purples, and greens—but the highest hues have private dwells." Kahalyton's eyes took on a distant look. His face was slack as if he were lost in memories of a distant time.

"Are all the dwells like this one?"

"Yes, except for the residences of the rainbows. During transit the rest of us have to move from one urbode to another and into a different dwell. Even the high hues move, but they don't have to share. The VIS and other white wristlock wearers, who all live in white urbodes, can return to their private dwells in the same urbode if they choose to do so. Shades like Ural and Mirall, who get enough jarva to bribe the best spotters, take possession of a new dwell as soon as the urbode is cleaned and opened. Then offer shelter to friends or foils who won't complain when the householder cuts their gruel."

"So that's what Ural is after. I've heard transit mentioned before. What is it?"

"Transit is the time of change when all colors except rainbows have to leave their old urbodes and find new dwells in different urbodes. Just as three shifts make a cycle, thirty cycles make a transit. On the first day of the new transit, all urbodes—except those that are limited to whites and rainbows and have a separate cleaning schedule—open their doors and stay open until the occupants leave. Even if they want to stay, they're forced to leave because everything in the urbode ceases to function. If any continue to stay the VIS arrests them. When the urbode is empty, the doors close for automatic cleaning and maintenance. The doors open after that and new occupants come in. The doors won't open to previous residents."

"How do people stay in touch with their friends?"

"The permanent grays use spotters and runners to keep track of new available locations and old associates. Those who stray too far from their compound during transit may or may not ever encounter anyone they knew before. Some grays use transit as a way of starting fresh, running or moving away from the old life. Most find that the newness gets old after fifty or sixty transits—especially for those who don't play the Game."

"Are there many urbodes where different colors live together?" I asked, thinking of Lyonella with her white wristlock.

"In a gray urbode only grays can key into the individual dwell identification system. A higher color can enter the urbode but can't get into any of the dwells without assistance. Not that many want to. The exceptions are rainbow and white wristlock wearers;

rainbows have universal access and whites have limited access. But there is very little mixing. Dedicated Game players don't have the time."

"What does a white wristlock signify?"

"White is the service color, worn by medics, clergy, helpers, and listeners. If the wristlock has black stars on the white band, the wearer is a member of VIS. Anyone can apply for a white wristlock after reaching the fifteenth level of the Game; some use a period of service as a timeout from the pressures of the Game. Service people are free to live in the lower thirty levels of any urbode; those who choose to live in urbodes that house only whites and rainbows have the privilege of continuing to stay in the same dwell at transit time."

Making certain that I wasn't being overheard, I asked, "What will I do at transit time?"

"Rathe, I'm a member of the Counter Colors, a political group working for the abolition of wristlocks, transit time and the VIS. You can join the movement and come with us."

I shook my head. "I appreciate your offer, but I'm too new to this world to commit myself to a political viewpoint and a system I know nothing about. I need more information and more experience to understand the situation."

"You've already got enough experience to know the system has serious flaws and stinks of corruption. The Counter Color movement needs you. Unlike the majority, you are open-minded, perceptive, alert and not addicted to the Game."

"But where would I go and what would I do?"

"Believe me; we have a place for you. We are better organized than anyone suspects. Remember, I found you; didn't I? For now, we want our enemies to underestimate us, but we have our own spotters, runners, busters, and other skilled people."

"Kahalyton, I don't know enough to be sure that I share your views. I know you're sincere, but I have to learn firsthand what this world is like before I can commit to changing it. I'm vaguely aware of your ideas; I know very little about your plans or goals."

Kahalyton's eyes burned like brilliant displays. "Once we have destroyed the color barriers, all people will be equal, naked before each other as on the day they left the House of Rebirth. We intend to create a new society based on equality and universal good will. We will abandon the Game in favor of pursuits that will benefit the new colorless community...."

Kahalyton's speech quickly degraded to rhetoric that I couldn't dispute or verify from my own shallow well of experience. I found myself tuning out, thinking of Lyonella while Kahalyton wound up his talk of glowing ideals and great changes.

After assuring me that he would see me again, he departed. I liked him better than the others I'd met so far, but I felt as if he viewed me more as a possible convert to the Counter Colors than a person or possible friend. I didn't know enough to have an opinion about this culture, but I preferred his impassioned fanaticism to the cold pragmatism of Errox. I wondered if I would have to choose between the two of them at the next transit.

They weren't my only choices. I could go to any gray dwell that would accept me and try to find my future in the Game. On the other hand, I wanted more from this existence than the dull existence that I had experienced so far with the grays.

Just before the second meal, Errox came to see me, acting friendly enough to make me suspicious.

He took a crystalline flask of greenish liquid out of a bag made from a tunic, offered it to me, and said, "Rathe, share a drink of jarva with me."

I took a sip. It went down smoothly, tasting like the purple food cubes, while warming my throat and stomach.

"Drink up," Errox said, as he took a deep drink. "I got jars and jars of jarva."

I downed another mouthful. Maybe it was the jarva that made Errox so friendly.

"Has anyone told you about the Simulike Palace?"

"No," I replied. "What is it?" The jarva had made me feel free to ask Errox questions. I took another drink.

"The Simulike Palace is where all things are possible. When you have the Simulike experience, your dreams, desires, and needs of the moment are fulfilled totally."

"Like in a dream?"

"It's as different from a dream as jarva is from water. It's as real as the taste in your mouth or the feel of a willing lover in your arms. You can exercise surprising powers. You can dominate or submit, create or even destroy. You can choose any man or woman for a lover and explore sex like never before."

My loins stirred with sexual excitement. The encounter with Lyonella bubbled to the surface of my mind. Errox and I both took another drink. Then I asked, "You've done this before? How did it make you feel?"

Errox's eyes glowed with a demonic gleam as he answered, "Like a god. There are no color bars in the world of Simulike."

"I might like to try that."

"Drink up, Rathe, and I'll take you to the nearest Simulike Palace."

We left Mirall's dwell and walked to the front slidestrip where we traveled to the main slideway. Hoping that the jarva hadn't befuddled me, I attempted to memorize Errox's route by counting pyramids and remembering directional changes after we left the original complex.

Errox maintained a friendly attitude but said little. We stepped onto a slower slidestrip and saw a large squat building which I suspected was the Simulike Palace. I was eager for the Simulike experience. Maybe this experience might jog my memory...?

As we approached the entrance, Errox said, "Don't tell the attendant that this is your first time. The procedure is simple. The attendant will lead you to a cubicle. There you lie down on the couch, fit the golden band around your head, and then put your arm in the right hand channel so that your wristlock fits in one of the grooves. The attendant will hypospray your left arm. From there on out, just relax and enjoy."

"How long will the Simulike experience last?"

"Longer than a meal, shorter than a sleep shift. It varies."

"How do I get back to Mirall's?" I asked.

"Whoever finishes first can wait outside for the other. Come on."

I eagerly followed Errox in. The attendant, who wore a white wristlock, took Errox to an empty cubicle and then led me to an adjacent one. I laid down, put on the golden headband and dropped my right arm into the channel so that my wristlock was in a groove. I felt the hypospray on my left arm. My awareness slowly drifted away....

*   *   *

When consciousness returned, I was leaning against a large cask in a narrow, dark tunnel. I heard voices from beyond a bend in the passageway. I understood the words although they sounded foreign to my ears. I cleared my throat.

The sound attracted a young woman in a flowing red dress who emerged from a side passage and said, "There you are. Come on. It's almost time for the ceremony to begin."

She took my hand and led me toward the voices. We entered a large chamber lit by smoky torches and pale yellow candles. Each torch illuminated a metal plate. Some of the plates had names engraved on them and others were blank.

The young woman and I took adjacent places along with ten others, all of us wearing red. We stood before a regal pair—a woman of incredible, ageless beauty and a handsome man with flowing white hair. The man said, "All the candidates are here."

The woman announced, "You are here before the priest and priestess of the tribe and in the presence of the other tribal members for the supreme initiation. Today the twelve of you will become torch bearers, keepers of the flame, sharing the enlightenment of the tribe of Eshkadella. The names you choose will be engraved upon our plaques illuminated by the torches that symbolize your new positions as fully initiated members of the tribe."

She turned to the priest beside her and said, "You may administer the sacraments."

The tall man dispensed small pieces of a dark brown root to the twelve of us and said, "Chew thoroughly before swallowing."

The tribal members standing around the perimeter of the chamber watched as we ingested the sacred plant, some sort of root. The taste was new to me, a pleasant bitterness.

After we were done chewing, the priest led us along a candle-lit path to an underground spring that bubbled up and flowed through a time worn channel across the cave floor and into the shadows. During the short walk I felt an incredible rush, as if something were dancing in my veins, floating joyously in my lungs, and fine-tuning all my nerve ends. Dizziness and gut rumblings were the side effects that we all shared.

"Kneel down by the channel and let it all come up," the priest ordered.

Within a short time, all of us threw up the contents of our stomach into the channel. As the spring water washed away all that we disgorged, the priest said, "The purification has begun."

When the vomiting ceased, the priestess said, "Rinse your mouths in the spring and be ready for the Dance of the Skeletons. Let the music begin."

Musicians, wearing green robes and conical orange hats, emerged from the ranks of tribal members. Their hollowed gourds, wide-bodied stringed instruments, bone xylophones, and hollow-log drums created a fascinating melody with a compelling beat. Tribal members thrust wired-together skeletons into our arms. The entire tribe chanted "Dance! Dance! Dance!"

Along with the other initiates, we whirled in frenzied circles, adding the rattling of a dozen skeletons to the spectacle and rhythm of the ceremony. The chanting tribal members herded us toward a small area that had twelve tunnels leading away from it. All the tunnels were narrow, dark, and foreboding. The music faded and the priest said, "Each candidate will enter a tunnel for the Communion of Flesh and Bone. When the candidates return, they will lay the Old Ones to rest in their crypts. Then each of the newly initiated will engrave a chosen name on a plaque."

Still lightheaded from the ceremonial root and the whirling dance, I entered a passageway. The floor was smooth as if worn down by human traffic over eons. When the light from the chamber no longer penetrated the passageway, I saw a solitary candle burning in an alcove. I approached the alcove and heard a female voice behind me say, "Hang the skeleton on the hook beneath the candle."

I relieved myself of the burden of the bones and turned toward the voice. Her face, indistinct in the candlelight, wavered in my drug-altered vision. First she appeared to be the woman in the red dress who led me into the big chamber for initiation. Then she became the beautiful priestess. Then she became every woman and I was in her arms, lost in lust and love. Clothes dropped like fall leaves, unneeded and unheeded. Rapidly, but without hurry, we began the communion of the flesh. I felt that everything I needed was mine and was sure that my chosen name would come to me when I needed to speak it.

Our mutual ardor multiplied until the world of our sensuality was all that existed. I took that world, compressed it into my scrotum. Then I allowed it to erupt and I felt like I had recreated the world from the union of flesh—

Suddenly, cold, hard hands ripped me from my bliss, grabbed me under the armpits and pulled me to my feet. I was dragged out of the Simulike cubicle by two men dressed in blue body suits and wearing white wristlocks with black stars. I saw Errox in the next cubicle; he was lost in the Simulike experience.

"What... What is going on?"

"Errox, 14893-2456331, we are the Variation Investigation Service. You are being taken into custody for social deviance and illegal entry."

I tried to reply, but a numbing fog was sprayed into my face. My will to resist drifted away....

SIX

When I regained consciousness, one of the burly VIS officers was locking a transparent collar around my neck. He saw that I was awake and asked, "You know what this is, Errox, don't you?"

"No."

"It's a custodial collar. You can't remove it unless you have one of these." He showed me a small box with buttons on it.

"With this disrupter," he said, "I can reduce the flow of signals to your brain. Any failure to cooperate in accompanying us to the nearest VIS center and I'll push this button and you will lose control of your mind and body. Would you like a demonstration?"

"No." I believed him. The old feeling of helplessness had returned in full force. I didn't need any demonstration of his power to know I was in bad trouble. By giving me his wristlock, Errox had transferred his identity, past sins and transgressions onto me.

With VIS officers on both sides of me, I was marched to the nearest slidestrip and was soon put into a VIS center detention cell, still wearing a collar. I hadn't bothered memorizing the route. There was a good chance I might never leave since I had no way of proving I wasn't Errox or anyone at all. Just a blanc, with no past, and now—no future.

The cell was small with walls as gray as my wristlock. I sat on one of the two built-in benches with my head in my hands. Nobody had informed me of any charges or what I was waiting for. I knew that I'd be questioned and, no matter what the questions were, my answers wouldn't be satisfactory.

If I told them I wasn't Errox, then I was guilty of wearing a wristlock that didn't belong to me. That would reveal that I was a blanc. Then I'd be sent to a holding center for nu-blancs where I suspected I would lose all my new memories. My memories weren't great, but they were all I had of my identity as Rathe—an identity I was determined to keep.

A small man, in a prim white tunic, entered my cell. He sat across from me on the other bench holding a disrupter for the collar locked around my neck.

"I am Arvon, the intake interrogator. Do you confirm your identity as Errox, 14893-2456331?"

"I have no answers for any of your questions."

"Do you deny that identity?"

"I neither confirm nor deny."

"We have identified you as Errox. You are suspected of illegal entry into the Color Wheel. You are suspected of being a riplocker and of associating with a subversive group. We are certain you are deviating from the social norms. You will have to be reconditioned. How deep that reconditioning goes depends on several factors; however, the single factor you control is your degree of cooperation. With verified cooperation you may be able to retain the socially acceptable portions of your character and personality. Do you understand that?"

"Yes."

"Then you will cooperate?"

"I refuse to answer any questions."

Arvon pressed the collar controller. My awareness dimmed out. I fell onto the floor. When I picked myself up, Arvon was gone. I had a headache and a skinned elbow. I lay down on the bench, wondering if I'd made the right choice.

The next time my cell door opened, a short brown-skinned woman with black hair and dark, piercing eyes entered. She wore the white wristlock with black stars that identified her as VIS, but no uniform. Her tunic was brown like mine. She held a collar disrupter in her hand.

"I'm Clandine, your custodian," she announced.

I didn't say anything.

She sat down on the opposite bench and waved the collar disrupter in the air. "Do you know the effects this can have?"

"Yes."

"Then you have no doubt who is in control here?"

"No doubts."

For a moment there was a faraway look on her face as if she were deciding something important before speaking. Then she said, "My priorities are different from Arvon's. He sees you as a potentially dangerous deviate from the norms. I see you as a potential agent of change. If a society can't adapt to positive change, it stagnates. In our society upward mobility is possible only by playing the Game and winning. But many people with talents and skills refuse to play the Game and remain grays."

"You are one of those people. You are skilled at survival and talented in dealing with others. You have influence and a reputation among many of the grays. I can get the charges against you dismissed if you act as my eyes and ears among the grays."

"I'm not a spy."

"I'm not asking you to betray associates. I need to know more about the resistance to rainbow rule. I know you're aware that a resistance group exists."

I knew I wasn't going to tell her anything about Kahalyton. He had been friendly toward me and I wasn't going to cause trouble for him and his Counter Colors. The look on my face must have revealed that I had some knowledge of the opposition.

Clandine quickly asked, "What do you know about the Freedom Crusaders?"

"Nothing," I answered, so surprised that the question wasn't about the Counter Colors that I replied without thinking about my intention not to answer questions. I suspected that Clandine was a more skilled interrogator than Arvon, perhaps skilled enough to get information I didn't want to give out.

Errox had saved my life, gotten me a wristlock, and taken me to a new dwell. Even though the wristlock had gotten me arrested by the VIS, I didn't know if that had been his intention. I wasn't sure what Errox had intended for me, but I knew he liked to have power over people. I had felt powerless ever since awakening in the Rainbow Room. Now, Clandine held the upper hand. She had the power to get my charges dismissed or punish me for Errox's sins—or my own.

"Errox do you know anything about a gray group that is recruiting volunteers from the permanent grays and using them to rebel against the system in dangerous ways?" she asked, her voice insistent.

"No. This is the first I've heard of them." I was getting information from Clandine's questions, but I couldn't fit what I knew into a cohesive whole. Kahalyton had spouted a lot of rhetoric about a utopian society that he envisioned, but he had told me nothing about how it was to be brought into being. I wondered if the Freedom Crusaders were a militant wing of the Counter Colors or a completely different group.

"I've heard that you have connections throughout the gray world. I was certain that you would know something about the strength of the Freedom Crusaders and how they condition their volunteers. You know they use terrorism as part of their means to challenge the social order?"

"I'm opposed to terrorism and if I had any information about terrorists I'd tell you."

"Look Errox, the Freedom Crusaders send members on suicide missions. I want to know how they recruit them and how they convince them to die in attacks upon the institutions and ways of our society."

"I don't know anything about them."

"You sound very sincere, Errox, and you project innocence well. I'm wondering if that is just part of your persuasive manner. You are much different from what I expected."

"What did you expect?" I asked.

"A smooth-talking confidence operator with greedy goals, superficial good looks, short term charm, and long term plans."

"I don't see myself that way."

"I haven't seen strong indications of those characteristics, either. You may be a better actor than anyone has ever suspected."

There was a rapping at the door. Clandine looked through the thick plastic window and then opened the door.

Arvon came in. He still looked neat and orderly but his manner was agitated. Arvon said to Clandine, "There must have been spotters outside the Simulike Palace. I just heard from a semi-reliable source that the Freedom Crusaders are going to attack this center to free the prisoners. I think that's because Errox is here."

"Are there any other prisoners here that you're sure are Freedom Crusaders?" Clandine asked.

"Five suspects. Errox makes six."

"We can't be certain they're after Errox. They could be interested in freeing one or more prisoners who are valuable to them—prisoners with an importance we haven't discovered yet."

"That could be," Arvon said. "I'll authorize a deep probe background check on the ones we aren't familiar with. If any of them are willing to cooperate, we can use the vericator to check their truthfulness. I've requested backup troops to deal with a possible Freedom Crusader attack even though I have limited confidence in the message from my informant.

"The threat of a Freedom Crusader attack may be just a ploy to get you to take Errox out of here. Then they would have a better chance of rescuing him or killing him if they think he knows too much. Either way you might get killed, Clandine."

"I'm not ready to leave here yet. If Errox tells us his story, I want to check it out with the vericator."

He turned to me and said, "If they're coming, they're probably coming after you. Do you know if it is to rescue you or to make sure you never talk? They have no compunction about taking the life of anyone for any reason or for what appears to be no reason at all. I don't understand them, but they're a potential danger to you. If you cooperate with Clandine, we may be able to save your life."

"If you destroy my personality with reconditioning, the life you save will not be mine. I don't see any difference between losing my identity and losing my life. Why should I cooperate in my own destruction?"

"Cooperation is the only way you can retain your identity, Errox," Clandine answered. "We have the techniques and the tools to brainwipe you, but doing that would mean we would never get the information you have. You can only help yourself by helping us."

"What does the brainwipe procedure do?"

"It destroys memory or access to memory. The subject retains motor skills, most of his language awareness and the basic human characteristics. It enables the candidate to start fresh after reorientation in an imprinting center."

Now I thought I knew exactly what had happened to me. I had been brainwiped and turned into a blanc. But I hadn't been taken to an imprinting center. I had been dumped in the Rainbow Room to die. The person I had been before I became Rathe must have had powerful enemies. I wondered who they were and if they were still my enemies.

"So my choices are retaining my knowledge of myself by cooperating or choosing not to cooperate and losing my identity."

"That's right," she replied. "I'll leave you in this cell to think it over while I check out the other prisoners suspected of being Freedom Crusaders."

They both left.

Alone in the perpetual twilight of my cell, I chased my own thoughts around in my head, unable to find any solution to my problems. I fell asleep on the bench. I don't know how long I slept. I awoke when a tray of food was passed through a slot in the door. The rations were about the same as the food in the two gray dwells where I'd had meals. It had been a long time since I had eaten. I finished every morsel. With a full stomach, I dozed off and on, seeking the prisoner's temporary relief from hopelessness and boredom.

The sound of the explosion and the shuddering of my cell brought me out of my stupor and into a chorus of noises—alarm bells, people yelling, doors opening and closing.

I looked out the plastic window in my cell door, wondering what had happened. All I could see were two VIS guards running by with their stunners drawn.

I smelled the gas before I felt its effects. It was seeping through the food slot, a yellowish brown haze that burned my throat and lungs. I blinked back tears as the gas poured through the door and slowly rose. I backed away from the door and got down on the floor taking shallow breaths where the air was cleaner.

I felt sluggish. My arms and legs seemed too heavy to move. I couldn't think straight. I tried to take only shallow breaths but even those seared my lungs. I didn't know if the gas was lethal or merely incapacitating.

I heard the door to my cell open. I looked up and saw two grays, a man and a woman, enter.

The man asked, "Is he Errox?"

The woman, after a cursory examination of my face, said, "No. Errox is shorter and stockier with gray hair."

"Errox wasn't in any of the other cells or offices. Where can he be?" asked the man.

The woman, already turned toward the cell door and headed back to the corridor, replied, "We've got the other Crusaders. It's time to go. Maybe Errox was never here. Maybe he escaped already. Come on."

They quickly left.

My cell door remained open. I marshaled my gradually returning strength and managed to climb onto a bench. The gas had dissipated but the air still held some of its stench. I could hear people moving and shouting in the hall. I went to my open cell door and looked down the long corridor that led to an exit.

The man who had entered my cell had a prisoner over his shoulders in a fireman's carry. The woman was right behind him.

Someone shouted, "There they go out the front portal."

The hum of what must have been five or six stunners filled my ears. The man was out and gone. The woman dropped like a puppet whose strings were severed.

I heard voices I couldn't identify. "They're all gone except her."

"No, there's a dead Crusader in the control room or what's left of him; he exploded his wristlock to damage the controls, committed suicide for the Crusaders' raid."

"How many prisoners are gone?"

"At least two. Maybe more."

"Get the medic for that woman. She might not survive those simultaneous stuns."

I'd regained enough strength to move. I looked down the corridor, wondering if I could get away in the confusion. Then the thought hit me—get away to where?

The only place I knew was Mirall's and I didn't know how to get there from here.

SEVEN

Clandine came to my cell, stepped through the still open door, saying, "I'm surprised you're still here, Errox. Why didn't you escape with the Crusaders? They could have cut off the custodial collar and you could be free to go where you want."

"I don't have any place to go."

"Do you think we implanted a tracer to use you as a Crusader locater?"

"I have nothing to do with the Crusaders."

"This was a suicide mission for the Crusader who used his wristlock to blow up the control room, but we captured another one. She's dying. I want you to hear her answer questions while hooked to a vericator. Come along."

I went with Clandine down several corridors and into a large room where a woman was stretched out on a medic cot. Standing nearby was Arvon.

A thin man with a white wristlock was attaching a skull cap and several sensors to the woman. The cap and sensors were connected to a screen display.

Clandine asked me, "Are you familiar with the vericator?"

"No, I don't remember ever seeing one before." After I said that, a fragment of memory about being hooked-up to a machine—maybe a vericator, maybe something else — drifted onto the main stage of my mind and then danced away. I tried to hold onto the image, even though it seemed unpleasant, but it was vague and elusive.

Clandine described the function of the vericator. "All data is fed into the enchancers in the display and analyzed. The line that shows up on the display represents the probability that the subject believes what she is saying—the higher the line, the greater the probability. There is no guarantee of truth, just an indication of whether she believes what she says."

I watched as the thin man made some adjustments. When he was satisfied, he nodded to Arvon.

"I'm Arvon," he said, looking direct only at the prisoner.   "Do you know that you are dying?"

The woman answered yes. The line on the display was near the top.

"Do you want us to attempt to save your life?"

"No, you'd just brainwipe me afterwards. I'll die a Freedom Crusader and be reborn in Freeland with the freedom lovers and all the other Crusaders who have given their lives for the cause."

I saw that she believed what she was saying. The believability linc hovered at the top of the display.

"Why did the Crusaders attack this VIS center?"

"To rescue Crusaders held here."

I didn't know how honest this Crusader had been previously in her life but she was telling the truth while dying. What she believed about being reborn in a special place made me think that she had been indoctrinated with unverifiable concepts and ideas that made her a fanatic. It seemed almost as bad as brainwiping to me. It caused me to wonder if the standard VIS conditioning induced the acceptance of dubious theories and practices. I turned my attention back to the questioning of the Crusader.

"Do you know Errox?" Arvon asked, without looking in my direction.

"He was my occasional lover for several transits." That was her truth and she seemed proud of it.

"Why didn't you rescue him?"

"We couldn't find him."

Clandine went over and whispered in Arvon's ear.

He nodded.

She motioned for me to come closer to the cot.

Arvon bent down, asking, "Do you know this gray in the collar?"

The Crusader looked me in the face. She said, "I don't know his name. I saw him earlier in a cell. I'd never seen him before."

The believability line never dropped, never wavered, remaining at the top of the display.

I saw the look exchanged between Arvon and Clandine. Now they knew I wasn't Errox. I released my breath in a heartfelt sigh unaware that I had been holding my breath. Although I was still a prisoner, I felt freer now that my captors were certain that I was not the person they had been seeking. I didn't have to carry the burden of a bogus identity any longer, but I didn't know if my situation had improved much.

The VIS knew who I wasn't, but now they knew I was guilty of wearing a wristlock that belonged to another person. Maybe this might cause them to uncover my former identity, helping me to learn what had happened to me and why.

Clandine took me back to my cell. Just before she locked the door, she said, "I'll be back later to collect you for your vericator session."

After she closed and locked the door to my cell, I wondered how much later it would be. Was Clandine waiting for the death of the Crusader so the vericator would be free or was this waiting designed to break down my defenses? Maybe it was both. My lack of memory was my biggest defense but no amount of waiting seemed likely to change that.

What did I really have to defend? Clandine knew that I wasn't Errox, but I was wearing his wristlock. That meant that I was involved in the illegal transfer of one wristlock. It didn't prove I knew Errox but since I hadn't protested being identified as Errox or claimed another identity, Clandine was probably sure that I knew Errox.

I didn't want to cause trouble for anyone, but I didn't think I could fool the vericator. I would have to avoid answering some questions if they were asked. Maybe I could volunteer truthful information that would interest Clandine without betraying anyone. The focus of the VIS was on the Freedom Crusaders. I could state that I knew nothing about them except what I'd learned here at the VIS Center and that would register as truth.

Since they hadn't asked about Kahalyton or the Counter Colors, I suspected they either didn't know about them or, if they knew, didn't consider them a threat. I didn't want to give them Hushel's name as the wristlock smitty who put Errox's wristlock on my arm. Even if Clandine was clever enough to elicit Hushel's name from me, I didn't know where his dwell was or how to look for it. Ignorance was my best defense.

The only dwell I knew how to get to was Mirall's, but I didn't know how to get there from here; I didn't know how to get anywhere from here. I wasn't aware that I'd dozed off until I was awakened by the sound of my cell door opening. Clandine was standing there, looking at me in a way that made me feel slightly uneasy, as if she knew something I didn't know. I wasn't sure what it was she knew but I wished I knew that, as well as the answers to all the questions that I hadn't asked of anyone.

Clandine led me to the room where the Crusader had been questioned. There was no sign of her. Arvon and the thin man were still in the room.

"Just lie down on the cot," she ordered.

I complied.

"Hook him up," she said to the thin man, who proceeded to attach the skull cap to my head and the other sensors to my body.

When he was finished, Clandine said, "Thank you, I'll take it from here."

The thin man left but Arvon stayed.

Clandine turned toward Arvon and said, "I want to be alone with the prisoner. I can establish a better rapport that way."

Arvon's face clouded briefly with anger, then returned to his normal impassive demeanor.

"Of course."

I could tell he wasn't pleased to be told to leave and I became aware of the power that Clandine wielded. As Clandine watched

Arvon leave, she asked an unexpected question, "Did you know that the wristlock you're wearing would identify you as Errox?"

"No," I replied.

I couldn't see the display but I knew I was telling the truth. Clandine seemed pleased, as if she'd gotten the answer she wanted.

"Are you a Freedom Crusader?"

"No," I answered, looking at Clandine's face to see if my answer altered her expression. It didn't.

"What do you know about the Freedom Crusaders?"

"Nothing except what I've learned here this cycle."

Clandine's mouth tightened in a disappointed look before she asked, "Do you know any Freedom Crusaders?"

"No, I never heard of them until I was brought here to the VIS Center."

I was beginning to feel comfortable with the questions. Clandine wanted information that I didn't have.

Then she asked, "What did you do with your previous wristlock?"

"I don't know?"

"What's your name?"

"Rathe."

"Rathe, was your previous wristlock gray?"

"I don't know."

Clandine looked pensive. She seemed to be mentally going over my truthful answers. She suddenly looked pleased and asked, "Are your earliest memories gone?"

"Yes," I replied.

That was the first positive reading she'd gotten from me and it was obvious that she felt she was onto something.

"Is Rathe a name that you remembered?"

"No."

"Do you remember anything from before you became a blanc?"

"No."

"Are you protecting Errox?"

I didn't know how to answer that, so I remained silent while I thought it over. Clandine appeared to be trying to interpret my silence. I wondered what showed on the display. Could the vericator show my confusion to Clandine?

"Do you know where Errox is?"

"No."

"Is Errox your friend?"

"I don't know." I knew that Errox had helped me but I couldn't be sure he was friendly toward me. He may have been planning to use me in some scheme that would benefit him. It was quite possible that Errox knew he was being searched for by the VIS and had gone to the Color Wheel for a new identity. I doubted he was perceptive enough to realize that a perfect stooge would also be waiting there. I'm sure that if he hadn't encountered me some other poor wretch would be undergoing interrogation.

"Do you think Errox gave you his wristlock only for your benefit?"

"I don't know."

Clandine shifted away from questions about Errox by asking, "Do you know how to find a wristlock smitty?"

"No, I don't."

"Could you find your way back to the one who put Errox's wristlock on your wrist?"

"No."

Clandine said, "I thought as much. Do you know anyone besides yourself and Errox who has gotten an unauthorized wristlock?"

"No."

"Rathe, I understand your situation. You were a blanc, knowing little about the life you found yourself in. Was Errox the first person you established a personal relationship with?"

"Yes."

"I can understand how you might feel a certain loyalty toward him, maybe even a friendship, but I can tell you that Errox has no friends. He only has business associates, minions, and people he thinks he can use. He is a riplocker, ripping off corpses for their wristlocks. You heard the dying Crusader say that she and Errox were lovers for a while. We don't know if he is a Crusader or not, but we do know that he knows some Crusaders. I want to find him and learn what he knows. Can you find him?"

"I don't know."

"Can I trust you to help me look for him?"

I couldn't answer that question. I guess my confusion showed on my face because the next thing she asked was, "Can I trust you?" I answered yes, probably because I wanted a relationship of trust. I had no memory of ever having had one but I wanted one desperately. I needed an anchor to diminish the free floating anxiety that had been my almost constant companion since I awoke in that dreadful Rainbow Room.

With an eager, earnest gaze into my eyes, Clandine said, "When I thought you were Errox, I told you what I wanted, namely someone who could help me find out about the Freedom Crusaders. I want to see that organization discredited and dismantled. They are suspected of illegally indoctrinating people, using the dangerous drug Cainenol to get volunteers for suicide missions and other potentially lethal activities. I need information. I can end your troubles with the VIS if you help me find Errox.

"I'm not looking to arrest him. I want to make him the same offer I made you—help me and I'll get the charges against you dismissed. I'm willing to meet him anywhere he feels safe and explain my proposition to him. You will not be betraying him. You will be aiding me in giving him the opportunity to erase his past missteps and begin again with a clean record. If you feel you owe Errox something, this is how you can repay him by giving him an opportunity to start afresh. What do you say?"

I found her argument convincing. I couldn't be sure what motives had prompted Errox to save my life and help me get located. This was an opportunity for me to do something for him while giving him the choice of whether he wanted this kind of help or not.

"What do I get if I agree?" I asked.

"All charges against you will be dropped and I'll make sure you get a wristlock and a place to live."

"I'm not sure I can find Errox. Does the deal still hold even if my efforts aren't successful?"

"Yes. Your cooperation is all I ask."

"The only place I know that Errox might visit is the dwell I was formerly living in. If I remember the route as well as I think I do, I can find my way there from the Simulike Palace."

"I'll get you disconnected from the vericator and we'll be on our way," she said, with the first smile I'd seen on her face.

Clandine left and shortly thereafter the thin man came in and removed the skull cap and the sensors.

I overheard Clandine and Arvon speaking in the hall. "I'm taking the ersatz Errox with me. Even though he isn't who we thought he was, he's the best lead I'm likely to get."

"It's almost time for first meal. I thought that you and I might discuss the case while eating."

"I can't take time to eat now," she said. "I'll keep you posted if anything significant happens. I appreciate your cooperation."

Clandine came in to collect me. She asked, "You don't mind missing first meal, do you? We can eat later. "

"I don't mind. I'm ready to go."

As we walked out of the damaged VIS center, a new day was dawning. I felt hopeful and optimistic.

EIGHT

Outside the VIS Center, Clandine removed the custodial collar and folded it into her waist pouch. We walked to the nearest slidestrip, I took a deep breath. The air was fresh and cool to my lungs, a welcome change from the gas-tainted atmosphere of the VIS Center. My collar was off. The rising sun seemed to hold the promise of a new and better day for me.

Clandine and I got on the slidestrip towards the nearest slideway. As we made our way toward the Simulike Palace, I asked her how she made her way around without directions. She said she'd developed a mental map that oriented her to the VIS Centers and all the other buildings like the Color Wheel and the Simulike Palace.

We got off a slidestrip at the Simulike Palace. It appeared to be closed at this early hour. The only people around were two grays sleeping on the walkway. As I looked at them I noticed that their limbs were trembling as if they were cold, although the early morning sun felt warm to me.

"Those two seem to be suffering from chills."

"It's probably a Cainenol reaction," she said.

"What's Cainenol?"

"An illegal drug. Take too much and the body can't handle it."

"Should we find a medic to treat them?"

"The twitching will go away without treatment, usually," she said. "The patrolling medics will find them if they stay here long enough to become a nuisance. But right now they're overworked and probably won't bother with them. The medics have enough problems trying to handle the Cainenol chumps who go berserk and attack everything, including each other."

I wondered if that was the drug that Lyonella had taken, possibly given to her by Vargan—possibly by me if I had been Vargan before I was brainwiped and turned into a blanc. I didn't want to let my thoughts linger on questions like that. Instead I told Clandine the route I remembered that would take me back to my dwell, the one place where we might find a way to get in touch with Errox. She listened with a concentration that made me certain that she was adding my information to the map in her head.

As we moved onto another slideway to follow the route I remembered, I saw some kind of commotion on the slowest strip. Clandine and I moved onto a faster strip to bypass the group who appeared to be fighting on the outside strip. When we got close enough to see what was going on, I could tell that it was a cluster of five or six people lashing out wildly at each other and at all the travelers who came within their reach.

"Watch out, berserkers are rioting on the slow strip," she said into a small handphone.

She pulled her stunner out of her waist pouch and, when she got close enough, began firing at the berserkers. Two of them, a woman with a torn tunic and a man with a bloody face, collapsed immediately. A second man with one eye swollen shut jumped off the slideway strip and ran down a walkway as if pursued by creatures from a nightmare.

A second woman jumped onto the slidestrip where Clandine and I were. She was a short distance behind us, running toward us in an adrenaline-charged rush of rage. I threw myself at her legs and knocked her off her feet.

Clandine pointed the stunner at the fallen woman and fired. The woman's eyes lost their crazed light and then the lids came down as if she were going to asleep.

"Help me pick her up," Clandine demanded.

I grabbed the woman under the arms and she picked up the woman's legs.

As soon as we had a firm grip on the unconscious berserker, Clandine said, "Let's move over to the slowest strip. We'll drop her off by a walkway. When she wakes up the berserker energy will be gone and she'll have a hangover but otherwise be okay."

After we put the woman down by the walkway, Clandine said, "If we had time, we could get on the fastest strip, catch up with the other two I stunned and get them off the strip, but we don't have time if we're going to catch the crew at your dwell during first meal."

I thought of the two downed berserkers on an unconscious trip to an unknown destination, doomed to arrive with a painful hangover and other body aches. I felt good by comparison until I realized that I'd lost count of how many urbodes we had passed and I had no idea where I was in relation to my dwell or the Simulike Palace.

"Clandine, I've lost count of the urbodes along this slidestrip. I don't know whether we've traveled too far or not far enough."

She nodded. "Then we'll have to go back to the Simulike Palace and retrace the route. I hope we can still get there by first meal. That's the best time to find most people at home."

We doubled back. There were more people on the slideway than there were earlier, but no more berserkers. I didn't let anything distract me from keeping the urbode count. We got off the slidestrip in front of the square of one hundred urbodes.

"My dwell is in the sixth row back from the front and is the fourth one on the left."

As we walked through the urbodes, more people came out of the front portals, some of them carrying a few belongings in bags made from old tunics, most of them carrying nothing that couldn't be kept in a waist pouch. Clandine looked at the exodus and said, "It's transit day. We better hurry or all the occupants of your urbode will be gone."

We arrived at the urbode only to find the front portal closed. In front were three grays—two men and a woman. Clandine said, "A spotter and a couple of runners. That means the building is empty for maintenance and they are waiting until the building opens again to notify the people they know who will be the new tenants. What was the name of the gray that Errox knew?"

"Miral."

We approached them. Clandine asked the woman, "Do you know where Miral went?" The woman looked at Clandine, saw the VIS white wristlock with the black stars and said, "There's no one left here from the building. They all left as soon as they finished first meal."

Clandine asked again, "Do you know Miral?"

"I don't know any Miral, and I don't know you."

Clandine turned to the two men and asked, "Do either of you know where Miral went?"

One man ignored her.

The other, a bald man of indeterminate age, said, "What do you want with Miral, whoever he is?"

Clandine answered, "I'm looking for Miral and a friend of his named Errox."

"We don't know them. If they used to live here they're gone, looking for new dwells. Who knows where? Not us. As soon as this urbode opens again, We're moving in along with a lot of others we know. We don't want VIS here. We've got busters coming to get rid of outsiders like you two. Leave now. There's nothing for you here."

Clandine turned away from the bald man and said to me, "We are too late. Let's go back to the slidestrip."

I was discouraged. If it hadn't been for the encounter with the berserkers, we might have gotten here in time to see Miral, or maybe even Errox if he came to visit.

I had hoped to help Clandine so that she would help me. Now, how could I help her? I had no dwell and no way to find one where I would be welcomed. I was a stranger in an unfamiliar land, wearing a wristlock that identified me as someone the authorities considered an undesirable, at best; at worst, a Freedom Crusader, part of a criminal conspiracy that caused death and destruction. I stopped walking, immobilized by my downward spiral of depressing thoughts.

Clandine halted, turned to me, and said, "While you were connected to the vericator, you told me I could trust you—and you were right. I've trusted you, but now it's time for you to trust me. You've got to tell me everything you know about Errox. Where did you first meet him?"

"In the Color Wheel."

"How did you get into the Color Wheel? Did Errox take you inside?"

"I woke up in the Rainbow Room of the Color Wheel. Evidently I'd been brainwiped and dumped there. Errox helped me get out alive."

"If you want my help, you've got to tell me everything. There's more to the story than you've told so far."

I hadn't wanted to relive that experience through recall and I didn't want to cause trouble for Errox but I needed help from Clandine. I felt that I owed Errox because he saved my life, but I owed more to myself—a satisfactory life and the opportunity to find out what happened to me and why. Somebody had me brainwiped and left in a place where I was intended to die. I was angry about that. I didn't just want explanations—I wanted revenge.

Clandine seemed my only chance now that Miral and the other grays had moved. Now she was my only contact in this nightmarish world. I decided to tell her everything that I knew about Errox. "I'll tell you what I know of Errox, but I won't let you use me as a witness against him. He saved my life. I owe him for that."

"Start from the beginning. What happened in the Rainbow Room?"

I told her the whole story—the wakeup call from the woman with the green wristlock, how she died, Errox's entrance through the exit, his removing the wristlock from the dead woman, my solving the Rainbow Room equation...

"You solved the equation and figured out which tiles would drop?" she asked, her voice rising.

"Yes, it was simple algebra."

"Errox knows you did this?"

I nodded. "He was there with me."

"Now I know why Errox saved your life. You weren't just another blanc. You were a person with brain power, someone that Errox could pretend to befriend and stash somewhere for later use. If you hadn't been picked up by that sweep of the Simulike Palace you can be sure that Errox had something else planned for you—like maybe an early death wearing his wristlock so the VIS wouldn't be looking for him anymore."

"I'm not convinced you're absolutely right, but I don't know anything that would prove you wrong."

"Errox did stash you in a dwell. Was it Miral's?"

"No. It was with someone else. I don't want to give you a name and cause trouble for that person."

"I don't need the name. Someone reported a nu-blanc who could play the Game well was staying at Ural's dwell. That was you. Ural has been under Errox's influence for some time. We don't know why, do you?"

"No."

"Since you're reluctant to name names, let me tell you that we know Errox deals with two smitties, Dreena and Hushel. Errox took you to a smitty's dwell, didn't he? There he had his wristlock replaced with the green one and had his old one put on you. Is that what happened?"

"Yes. It happened just like that. Then he took me to Miral's. The next time he came by, we went to the Simulike Palace. You know what happened after that?"

"What did you experience while under Simulike?"

"The experience was completely real. I found myself being initiated into full membership in a tribe with mind-changing sacraments and strange rituals that were to culminate in a naming ceremony."

"That figures," she said. "You were getting what you needed: acceptance and a name, a feeling of belonging. That's what the Simulike is supposed to do—create a fantasy that meets your needs. Was there any violence in the scene, directed toward you or anyone else?"

"No," I replied.

"That's a good indication that you would never make a good Freedom Crusader. If you believed that might makes right, you would have had an encounter with enemies and killed them."

"I wouldn't hesitate to defend myself if attacked," I interjected.

"I believe you, but your Simulike experience shows that you are not full of the kind of rage that the Crusaders want to nourish and channel. I think it's very possible that Errox took you to the Simulike Palace to learn more about you. Once he learned what you needed, he would be in a position of increased knowledge and greater power. Errox probably intended to use your brain power and your abilities to improve his position in the world."

"You make him sound like a monster."

"Isn't he? From what I know, Errox is one of those people who has never known love, never recognized the meaning of any life but his own. He uses people, takes rights for himself that he denies to others. He can murder, torture and mutilate because he has never felt empathy. He regards other people as animate objects for manipulation."

"He may have been manipulating me, but he did save my life. Then, he helped me obtain food and shelter. I don't have either now."

She looked up and down the slidestrip. "Come on. There's nothing for us here. Let's get on the slidestrip and go."

"Go where? Transit time has robbed me of any place to go."

"We'll go to my dwell. I promised I'd get you something to eat. You can stay with me for the time being."

It was the best offer I'd had today; it wasn't likely that I'd get a better one. As far as I knew, I'd never had a better offer in my life. But maybe I was still in custody. Clandine knew that she could trust me. I'd told her so and my words had been verified by the vericator. I wished I knew how far I could trust Clandine. I know that she had originally wanted to use me as a spy. Maybe she still did? Had I given her more power over me by telling her about my Simulike experience? I hadn't told her about the sexual content of my initiation because I wasn't sure whether or not she would use sex to try to control me.

I said, "Lead the way." I was tired of my own thoughts but not so tired that I neglected to add the route to Clandine's dwell to my mental map.

NINE

Clandine's dwell was in an urbode not far from the Simulike Palace. I added its location to my mental map as a permanent landmark since Clandine, as a white wristlock wearer, did not have to change residences on Transit Day. Her dwell was cleaned on a separate schedule, saving her from the reorientation that most people went through every thirty cycles. *This world would be far more pleasant*, I thought, *if all the urbodes could be cleaned on a schedule that didn't require the tenants to find new lodgings.* My mental musing stopped when Clandine spoke.

"Sit down, Rathe. We'll have a late first meal."

The food was the same as I'd had in the other urbodes and in the VIS center, but it seemed better here because there were only two of us and we were in a comfortable setting.

"I'm sorry that we couldn't find Miral or Errox," I said. "I didn't know that it was Transit Day nor did I have any idea how disruptive it would be. I can understand the need for cleaning urbodes and that the people need to be out during the process but why do all the people, except the rainbows and some of the whites, have to change dwells?"

With a serious look on her oval face, Clandine said, "Transit Day forces the players of the Game to take a break and keeps some of them from burning out. It gives the white wristlock wearers that have to move—like Listeners and Clerics—a renewal and all new clients until the next Transit Day. It also makes it more difficult for grays to form permanent groupings. It's like True Faith Forever, another device for controlling grays."

"Some of the grays in my last urbode tried to interest me in meeting with a Cleric," I said. "The idea of devoting this life to spiritual exercises in order to have a better next incarnation requires more faith than I have."

"Me too," Clandine said. "I don't want to waste this life on speculation. I'm trying to improve things so that when I emerge from the House of Rebirth for my next life I'll find the world a better place, even if I don't remember what it was like before."

"Is it true that only rainbows retain their memories when they reincarnate?" I asked.

"Rainbows don't pass through the House of Rebirth. When they want their life renewed they go to the Fane of Change and come out rejuvenated with memory intact. Immortality! All you have to do is play the Game."

There was a note of dissatisfaction or disbelief in Clandine's voice that I hadn't heard before. I asked, "Why don't you play the Game?"

"I wanted to do something better with my life. I wear the white wristlock of the VIS because it gives me the power to help root out the misguided and criminal elements in our society. I want to stop the Freedom Crusaders. They're tied into the distribution of Cainenol, the drug that's becoming a plague on our society. The Crusaders use it to control the minds of recruits, convincing them that if they die in the cause of freedom they will be reborn in a paradise called Freeland. Some of the recruits die from overdoses and some have berserker reactions. I want to stop the flow of Cainenol."

"Do you think Errox is involved in supplying the drug?"

"I don't know but I think he could find out about it. He might be willing to do that to get his slate wiped clean instead of being brainwiped."

From the way she talked, I realized that Clandine would have no compunctions about brainwiping anyone who didn't cooperate with her. Knowing that, made me uneasy. I hoped I had the skills to appear useful to Clandine until I could find a way to get out of her custody. I wasn't wearing the control collar, but I was still under her watch. I needed to know more about Transit Day if I wanted to survive until the next one. But, first, I needed to find a new dwell.

"I can see the kind of problems you're dealing with, Clandine, but doesn't Transit Day complicate things for you, even though you don't have to move?"

"Yes, but that's never going to be easy to change since Transit Day promotes the Game. As long as most of the best people concentrate on the game, the rainbows will continue to run things and whites perform the necessary services that can't be automated. Friends and acquaintances may lose track of each other every transit, but the Game goes on forever."

"Why is the Game so crucial? I played it once for a few minutes and I found it interesting because I was good at it. It didn't seem to be important enough to be the center of my life."

"The Game allows everyone a chance for upward mobility. People who are good at symbol manipulation and pattern detection advance to higher levels of the Game where the solutions of abstractions provide the skills the rainbows need to govern and control this world."

All at once, I understood what Clandine was trying to tell me. The Game served two purposes: it kept the best and brightest involved in producing data that preserved the system, while keeping those who didn't play the game in a position of powerlessness.

"The permanent grays get food, shelter, and clothing," I said, "but they have no hope for anything better, no chance to advance unless they play the Game and win—and they can't or won't. So the main job of the VIS is to make sure the permanent grays don't get organized and try to change things. Is that correct?"

"It's true that most VIS personnel are working to resist change. I'm not against change as a matter of policy, but I only want changes that improve society. That makes me one of the few who realize that controlled change can benefit our world, but unthinking resistance to all change can promote stagnation, decay, and destruction."

"You said you are one of the few. Does that mean that there are others who share your perceptions, and possibly your goals?"

"Rathe, you told me I could trust you and the vericator verified that statement as truth. But there is another reason why I think you're trustworthy—you were a blanc a short time ago; you haven't had time to become part of the conspiracy."

"What conspiracy?"

"I believe that some of the rainbows have banded together to control or manipulate the Game to increase and maintain their power."

"Rainbows already have all the real power in this society, don't they?"

"True, but some of the rainbows are doing things that indicate that they want more power than they have now. The rainbows who oversee VIS operations appear to have put obstacles in the way of the VIS personnel who are trying to control the flow of Cainenol. I suspect those rainbows are either involved in the drug trade, have friends who promote the drug or want to use the disruption the drug causes as an excuse to take greater control over VIS policies and personnel. I need your help in investigating this situation."

"My help? I can't even help myself. I don't have a dwell and the wristlock I'm wearing belongs to a suspected criminal."

Clandine looked deep into my eyes, "Rathe, I need someone who isn't part of VIS, someone to obtain information that you might be able to get. My VIS wristlock makes people suspicious when I ask them questions."

"Where and how would I get any useful information?" I had already been burned while acting as Errox's cat's-paw, so I wasn't anxious to follow the same path with Clandine.

"I have some suspects in mind that you can approach."

"Clandine, I'm not sure I know enough to convince anyone to give me information that would help you."

"One of my suspects is a Listener. Do you know what a Listener does?"

"Listen, I guess."

"Right," Clandine said, rewarding me with a smile. "A Listener provides that service. Anyone can go to a Listener and talk about problems. The Listener may give advice, give the person some things to think about, or merely assure the person that the Listener has heard and understood. Mostly Listeners deal with grays who don't play the Game or others who want to know if they can become Listeners. I want you to tell your story to my Listener suspect and tell me whatever she tells you. Her name is Lyonella."

I tried my best to keep the shock I felt off my face. Did Clandine know that I had met Lyonella and that *she* believed we had a past?

"One of my associates will check to see where her dwell is when Transit Day is over. Once we locate her, I'll tell you how to get to her dwell, and then you can get her to listen to your story."

"My story?" I was surprised to learn that Lyonella was a Listener. My previous experience with her had made me aware that she was a confused person, someone whose grip on reality wasn't very strong. If she didn't know already, I didn't want to let Clandine know that I had encountered Lyonella before.

"Yes, your story. You tell her about waking up as a nu-blanc in the Rainbow Room, solving the equation, and escaping. You tell her about being befriended by a gray who made sure you had a dwell and a wristlock. Tell her about your Simulike experience, then being arrested by the VIS and being placed in my custody—"

"You want me to tell her about you?" I asked. "Won't that make her suspicious of me?"

"I don't think so, Rathe. I don't think she knows that anyone suspects her of being part of the conspiracy. Besides, it's her duty as a Listener to hear you out. You can tell her that you're not sure you can trust me; although I've promised you a wristlock of your own and a dwell. Let her know that you're staying with me and you're still wearing the wristlock of a suspected criminal. Whatever she tells you will give me more information to work with."

I was willing to give Clandine's plan a try. Telling my story to a Listener might have a certain therapeutic effect; although, Lyonella would have been my last choice as a personal Listener—had I a choice in the matter... Thinking about Lyonella aroused mixed feelings. In our previous encounter her sexuality had almost overwhelmed me. Would that happen again? She could make me want her sexually, but I didn't want to enter into a relationship unless I could be sure we shared a little more than unbridled lust.

On the other hand, would Lyonella still insist that I was someone she'd known as Vargan? If so, maybe she could tell me about myself and my previous life and identity? Or was she just mentally disturbed, as she'd appeared? It was possible she had confused me with someone else or invented our past relationship? I needed to find out. I knew I could tell my story and make it sound real—especially the part about not being sure I could trust Clandine.

I found Clandine's great conspiracy theory possible but not necessarily probable. I knew that she, like Errox, intended to use me for her own ends. Her commitment was to her theory, not to me. Regardless, I was going to do it because I wanted to do something about my situation and this was the only path of action open to me where I would have some support. I told Clandine, "I'll give it my best effort."

"Good. I'll rehearse you in the part you'll play. Because I'll want you to tell almost the same story to one of my rainbow suspects, whichever one you can find at home on All Hues Day."

"Almost the same story? And what is All Hues Day?"

"You'll tell the rainbow that you overheard two grays in an urbode say that he or she was one of the few rainbows who was reputed to be concerned about the gray population. Then you'll explain your situation briefly and ask for help or advice. Whatever you learn, you can pass back to me."

"How will I get access to a rainbow?" I asked.

"They usually stay in their dwells on holidays because holidays are designed to keep the rest of the population in line. The next holiday is All Hues Day, a day off from the Game. The Game controls are turned off. All the public buildings—like the Simulike Palace and the Color Wheel—are turned into celebration sites where the clergy and other volunteers serve holiday food and jarva punch. All levels of every urbode are open to everyone. The clergy emphasize the spiritual aspects of the holiday, a chance for volunteers to understand the spirituality of service.

"The Game players are forced to take a day off; many of them relieve their tensions with jarva and casual sex in a carnival atmosphere. Some of the rainbows participate in the pleasures of the senses. During All Hues Day you should be able to make contact with one of my rainbow suspects—just one, because they might compare experiences and get suspicious of you, if you told your story to more than one of them."

"I guess I can do that convincingly."

"Sure you can," she said reassuringly. "You can get an early start on All Hues Day, report back to me, and still have time to enjoy the holiday yourself. It's not a holiday that I celebrate, so I'll be here at my dwell whenever you can get back with a report."

I believed I was beginning to learn more about Clandine. Her power in the VIS made me suspect that she was a dedicated high-achiever and her conspiracy theory might be the result of paranoid tendencies. Her lack of interest in the sensual aspects of All Hues Day was an indication that she wasn't interested in casual sex and sensuality. That probably meant she wouldn't initiate a sexual relationship with me as a control ploy. That was all right with me. I didn't want the relationship to get any more complex than it already was.

I felt that I could trust Clandine to make the best use of me that she could. I wanted her to be pleased enough with me to provide me with a wristlock and a dwell. I wasn't sure that she would until she got confirmation of her conspiracy theory, which may or may not have any basis in reality. Regardless, she was my best hope for a better life. So I told her, "I'm ready to rehearse my story whenever you're ready."

TEN

The next day Clandine shared more details of her mental map. "You have to know your way around so you can find Lyonella's dwell as soon as I learn where she is. Here's a pixcube that holds a likeness of her. Study it so you'll recognize her when you see her."

I looked at the pixcube and saw a three dimensional image of Lyonella. The image was accurate, displaying her tall, slim body with good muscle definition; her triangular face with the knowing expression and the haunted brown eyes that appeared to have seen more than I could imagine. I felt an inadvertent rush of blood to my groin: Lyonella's sensuality had been captured by the pixcube.

"Is something wrong?" Clandine asked.

I was still hoping that I wouldn't have to tell Clandine that I'd encountered Lyonella previously. "No, I'm just concentrating to make sure that I'll recognize her when I see her."

"I should get the location of her dwell today from the rainbow who oversees the Listener Guild. After third meal, I want you to try to arrange a listening session with her. I want you to be ready with your story as we rehearsed it."

"I'll be ready." I had mixed feelings about seeing Lyonella again. If she accepted me as just another gray, who wanted to tell her the story of his troubles, I'd be all right and I could tell

Clandine whatever Lyonella said. But, if Lyonella identified me as Vargan, there might be several kinds of trouble. If I had been Vargan before I was brainwiped, I didn't want Clandine to know that, just like I didn't want her to know I'd encountered Lyonella previously. Clandine might think I had been or was now some part of the grand conspiracy that she perceived. I thought it quite possible that she was a bit paranoid, seeing a power-grabbing conspiracy where there might be none.

The rainbows and her other suspects were people with power; they might not be in a conspiracy at all. Just merely indifferent to those who posed no threat to their positions and activities.

*   *   *

Later in the day, Clandine returned with Lyonella's location. When she was sure I knew how to get there and had my story straight, I headed toward Lyonella's dwell, hoping that all would go well.

Clandine told me that the most direct route to Lyonella's dwell involved going to the Medical Complex and walking through to the opposite side. I took three different slideways to reach the Medical Complex. It was a refreshing change to see buildings that were shaped differently from the ubiquitous urbodes. I followed the walkways through the cluster of buildings, heading for the slidestrip on the far side.

I passed the Rejuvenation Center, a tall oval building, where the sick and injured were taken to be healed or readied for reincarnation. It was next to the House of Rebirth where citizens were reborn without their memories into young and healthy bodies, ready to begin a new life. In the distance I saw the Fane of

Change where aging rainbows went so they could emerge with their bodies reconditioned and their memories intact—eternal life with periodic renewal.

I envied the rainbows their retention of memory. I felt I could lose that envy only by becoming a rainbow myself. I had hopes. I'd been good at the Game when I played it in Ural's dwell. If I managed to get a wristlock of my own instead of wearing one that identified me as Errox, I'd play the Game again. Maybe I could become a rainbow and hold onto my memories forever.

I took the slideway on the far side of the complex to a section of one hundred urbodes, got off, and counted my way to the urbode in which Lyonella lived. The entrance portal was guarded by the same tough-looking woman who had been at the door of the urbode where I'd gotten Errox's wristlock, the urbode where Hushel and Lyonella both had dwells. I remembered Lyonella had told me she would be near Hushel.

I supposed that Hushel, Lyonella, and many others had moved from the former urbode to this one on Transit Day. I stooped down in front of the portal guard and said, "I'm here to see Lyonella the Listener." With her hands, she indicated the floor and dwell number. Then she motioned for me to enter. I pressed the wristlock against the door plate. The door opened and I entered. I passed a few grays in the corridor, all strangers to me.

I stood at the door to Lyonella's dwell. I wondered what kind of a reception I'd get as I pressed my wristlock against the dwell plate. Nothing happened. Either Lyonella was not home or was not answering her door. I waited in the corridor for a while and then tried again with no results.

Finally, I left the urbode. Outside I went straight ahead and took a position across the walkway where I could watch the entrance, hoping that Lyonella would return soon. My waiting paid off. While it was still twilight I saw Lyonella, not entering the building but leaving it. I followed her. I told myself that I was following her in order to get more information for Clandine, but I knew that part of my motivation was the physical attraction I felt for her.

Lyonella went to a portal slidestrip leading to the slideway. Her loose-limbed, hip-swinging walk was a pleasure to watch, so different from the tightly controlled movements of Clandine. I made certain that there were always several people between us. I was counting on that and the fading twilight to prevent her detecting that she had a follower. Lyonella changed slideways. I followed close behind, keeping an eye on her and keeping track of my changing location on my mental map. I was surprised when Lyonella got off the slidestrip in the autofactory section.

There were few slide riders around. I tried to keep in the shadows as I followed her off the exit slideway and down a long passageway between two humming buildings. Ahead I could see the passageway ended at an entrance to a short, apparently square building with open doors. A giant of a man, more than a head taller than me, stood outside the door.

Lyonella had a brief conversation with him. He handed her what looked like two strips of tunic cloth. I saw her tie one over her wristlock and the other around her head like a headband for her shaggy hair before she went through the door. I hadn't come this far to turn back. I walked up to the giant, wondering if there was a password or some other sort of identification required to enter. I wanted to know what Lyonella could possibly be doing in the autofactory sector. As far as I knew all the factories were automated.

As I approached the giant, he said, in a rumbling bass, "The woman you are following said it was all right for me to admit you." He handed me a strip of tunic and said, "Tie this around your wristlock."

I took it and covered my wristlock. He handed me another strip of tunic and said, "This is your mask." I saw the piece of tunic had two holes for my eyes and a triangular notch cut out between them for my nose. I put the mask on.

The giant said, "Enter and enjoy freedom."

Freedom! What a dangerous word. Had I stumbled into a gathering of Freedom Crusaders? Maybe Clandine was partially right in suspecting Lyonella of involvement in a conspiracy. I looked at the entrance, obviously intended to admit machines larger than people, machines the size of walkway washers and slidestrip sweepers. I saw jumper wires attached to the alarm circuits.

Someone had outsmarted the devices intended to keep people out of the factory buildings. It was too late to turn back. I went in. The lingering twilight didn't penetrate all of the building, an edifice that had obviously been designed strictly for machines. On each side of the wide center aisle there were bins the size of large rooms, which held varying amounts of material. The bin nearest me held a variety of metal parts, some of them obviously damaged. I recognized some bent pieces of a walkway washer, a broken Simulike headband, and a damaged wristlock machine. Maybe this was where Hushel's machine had come from—a broken machine repaired by human hands instead of mechanical ones.

I walked down the wide aisle toward one of the room-like bins on the left where flickering shadows and rhythmic drumming indicated the presence of people. The drumming was pervasive. I found myself walking to its beat without having made a conscious decision to do so. My first look at the people inside revealed that they were wearing masks and wristlock covers, as I was. I focused on the drummers at the rear, partially visible in the light from a fire bowl in the center of the room.

The smell of the smoke was unfamiliar but agreeably piquant. Through the smoke I was able to make out a dozen drummers, using hands or implements, beating out rhythms on a variety of instruments fashioned out of the damaged materials from the storage buildings. I saw several clusters of people sitting on piles of old tunics and a handful of dancers, both men and women, dancing individually to the hypnotic beat of the drums.

Among the dancers was Lyonella. Although the mask partially hid the expression on her face, she seemed completely absorbed in her own movements. I lost track of time as I watched her sensual movements, the suppleness of her limbs, the sureness of her grace. She seemed like a different person than the disturbed woman who had taken me to be Vargan. She saw me watching her. She danced toward me, beckoning for me to come to her, my invitation to the dance.

Captivated by her allure and the pervasive beat of the drums, I found myself moving within her reach, matching her movements as best I could, reveling in the physical joy of expressive dance. I turned, whirled, dipped and pranced, feeling the gloriousness of being part of a creative whole. The drumming slowed and then stopped.

Lyonella took me by the hand and led me toward the left wall where bottles of jarva were being passed and shared. Lyonella and I both drank from the same bottle as if in a symbolic union of unknown dimensions. We sat on a pile of tunics. In the glow of the firebowl I could see a thin sheen of perspiration on her forehead above the mask. I took a deep breath and smelled her sweet muskiness.

"Enjoying your freedom?" she asked.

I had almost forgotten my suspicion that this gathering might be a function created by the Freedom Crusaders. I wondered if Lyonella was part of the conspiracy and if she was trying to recruit me.

"What freedom do you mean?"

"Freedom of the mask. Your face is masked, your wristlock concealed. You're free to be. You followed me, but didn't feel free to approach me. I told the door guard to let you in because I wanted you to be free, free to tell me what you want from me."

"I want you to listen to my story and give me advice."

"Be free, Stranger. You want more than advice. I can feel your want."

As she said that, Lyonella put one hand on the cloth covering my wristlock, the other hand over my heart, and rested her forehead against my own.

"I...I feel your wristlock is wrong for you—not in tune with your heart or your head. The dance didn't loosen all your tension. You want me and yet you're hesitant to act. Don't be wary. Don't talk."

She pressed her smooth, full lips to mine. Her tongue sought and found a gateway between my lips that allowed her to explore my mouth. I put my arms around her and drew her even closer. The touch of my hands on her skin was electrifying. I felt fully alive and held her as if I never wanted to let her go. My heart was beating in sync with the drums. I hadn't been aware they had started playing again. I was enveloped in a sensual universe where there were only the two of us.

We burrowed into a pile of tunics as if making a nest, eased out of our own tunics and pressed flesh upon flesh. Her small, round breasts flattened against my chest. I pulled back to touch one gently with my fingertips. When her nipple hardened, I took it between my lips and tenderly teased it with my tongue. Her hand moved from my neck and began a sensual journey to my abdomen. She found me ready and guided me into the union of opposites.

We moved with the beat of the drums. In the flickering light I could see the smile of her mouth. Her mask eyeholes were two shadows and I could not tell if her eyes were open or closed until a shift of the tunics which we were nesting in let a beam of light illuminate her soft brown eyes which were looking directly into mine. I felt my essence escaping my body as I experienced a thundering climax.

I'm not sure whether or not I lost consciousness but when I was able to think again, I could only think of Lyonella and the experience we had just shared. We stayed entwined for another timeless moment until the drums stopped and someone said, "There's jarva for everyone."

We put on our tunics. I asked her, "Do you want some jarva?"

"Not especially. Do you?"

"I don't feel I need anything."

She smiled at me and then a more serious expression settled on her face. She said, "I think I need to listen to you. Your body is at rest but your mind remains restless. Tell me what led you to seek my advice."

Reality came rushing back—the Rainbow Room, Errox, Ural, a disturbed Lyonella, Hushel, Miral, the Simulike Palace, the tribal initiation interrupted by the VIS, the Freedom Crusaders attacking the VIS Center, Clandine and her disciplined ways—I had to have something to tell Clandine.

"I was brainwiped, stripped of my wristlock and dumped in the Rainbow Room to die. I survived. I managed to get a wristlock but it belonged to someone wanted by the VIS. The VIS took me into custody. I'm in a dwell with a VIS officer who says she'll get me a wristlock if I help her. I don't know if I can help her and I don't know if I can trust her to help me."

Lyonella's face took on a trancelike look as she closed her eyes and said, "Change wristlocks at the first opportunity. Never play the Game. The Game is not what it seems. The VIS officer can be trusted only as long as she can use you. Her suspicions await transformation. Be of use if you can."

I memorized every word she said.

Lyonella opened her eyes and said, "I get veiled future images. They're gone now. I hope I've helped you."

"Will I see you again?" I asked.

"Yes, but go now."

"I'll cherish this memory of tonight. It's the best memory I have."

"I know but now you must go," Lyonella said in a soft voice. "My gift tells me there is danger in the cycle ahead for us both, but more if we're together."

As I walked back to the door to leave, it felt as though my feet were hardly touching the ground. The world seemed like a better place now than it had been before.

ELEVEN

I didn't tell Clandine about following Lyonella or about the scene in the factory area. I did tell Clandine that Lyonella didn't answer her door when I got to her dwell, that I had waited until she appeared and that Lyonella had listened to me and advised me.

Clandine asked, "Did you tell her that you weren't sure you could trust me?"

"Yes. Just like we rehearsed it. She told me I could trust you to the extent that I can help you confirm your suspicions."

"What else did she tell you?"

"She told me to get a new wristlock, but never play the Game."

"Did she give you a reason?" Clandine asked her forehead furrowed.

"She said the Game is not what it seems."

"What did she say it was?"

"All she said was not to play it and that it wasn't what it seemed."

A perplexed look remained on Clandine's face as she asked, "Why do you think she warned you about the Game?"

"I asked her for advice. That's the advice she gave me. She seemed sincere. I didn't question her about her answers. She's not as verbal or as orderly as you are."

"I think she must have a hidden purpose in telling you the Game is not what it seems and not for you. She wants you to be doing something else, something that might be of benefit to her and her associates, but not necessarily to you."

"I know you suspect Lyonella, but I don't know why."

"I'm almost certain she is part of the power conspiracy. Some of her clients have joined the Freedom Crusaders; others have vanished. I think she violates the Listeners Guild code by repeating some of what she hears to others. Did she do or say anything to make certain that you'd see her again?"

I flashed back to our sexual encounter; I didn't think it would be wise to mention that to Clandine. I need my own privacy and was still uncertain about Clandine's trustworthiness. I hoped that Lyonella's motives were as open as they had appeared to be. "No, she didn't even ask me my name."

"Maybe she already knew it."

"She didn't call me by it or invite me to have another listening session."

"Don't try to defend her," Clandine snapped.

"I'm not. I'm just telling you what happened. If she's part of a conspiracy, she's a cautious actor or a very subtle one."

"Yes, that could be it. It's late. Let's get some sleep and tomorrow I'll brief you about what's next. On All Hues Day you'll be mixing with the rainbows."

I didn't have any trouble going to sleep. I hoped to dream of Lyonella but, if I did, I didn't remember my dreams.

The next morning, after first meal, Clandine showed me pixcubes of three of her rainbow suspects.

"I want you to contact only one of these three suspects. As I said before, they know each other and might get suspicious if more than one of them met you. Which one you talk to depends on which one you find at home first."

The first pixcube was of a man Clandine identified as Flantel, overseer of the Clerics Guild. The pixcube showed a tall, large man. His thick torso was topped by a large head with pale blue eyes and almost colorless blond hair. Clandine said, "Flantel presents himself as a spiritual person, but I have suspicions that he is more interested in personal power and the pleasures of the flesh. I think some of the more corrupt clergy provide him with information about grays who are dissatisfied and of possible use to him. His dwell is near the Color Wheel. He will probably be home on All Hues Day."

Her mention of the Color Wheel brought back a memory of the danger I faced there. I asked, "What should I say to him?"

"Tell him that you have sought him out to ask if he has any special spiritual program for someone like you who is trying to develop his spirituality, but is handicapped by a blanc background and by the lack of a proper wristlock."

"Do you think he'll believe that? What if he turns me into the VIS?"

"I've thought about it," Clandine said, "from what I know of him, it's very likely that he will believe your story. Even if he is suspicious, Flantel will act as if he believes you because that is part of his image. At worst, he will probably suspect you of no more than an attempt to get a wristlock from someone who might be sympathetic to your plight. As far as turning you over to us, I believe he has more reasons to be cautious than you do."

Her reasoning had certain logic to it. I hoped she was right. Clandine showed me another pixcube and said, "This is Boget, the overseer of the Simulike Palace. His dwell is adjacent to the Palace. He monitors the experiences of the Simulike users. I think he has convinced some of them to serve him in illegal ways. I suspect that he is involved in Cainenol distribution."

The pixcube was of a handsome man with black hair and bright blue eyes. He was smiling as if demonstrating his good will toward the world. He, like Flantel, was someone I had never seen before—at least not since I had become Rathe. "What kind of a story do I tell him?"

"Tell him about your Simulike experience and how you were arrested by the VIS because the wristlock you wear belongs to a suspected criminal. Tell him the VIS released you from the center once they realized you were not the person they were looking for. Ask him if there is any way he can help you get a legitimate wristlock so you can have the Simulike experience without the potential problem of being arrested again by the VIS."

"I shouldn't have any trouble making that believable. I'd very much like to be able to visit the Simulike Palace again."

Then Clandine showed me the third pixcube. It was of a woman whose charisma I felt just looking at her image in three dimensions. She was of medium height with a wiry body. She had pale blonde hair that fell across her high forehead in geometric perfection. Her eyebrows had a high arch. Her eyes were a deep gray and her gaze was almost hypnotic. The skin of her face was stretched tightly over a prominent bone structure. There was very little flesh in her cheeks. Her jaw line was almost square. The overall effect was striking; yet she appeared hauntingly familiar.

It was possible that I may have seen her somewhere recently, but I suspected she might have been part of the memories I had lost when brainwiped. Then again, it might be wishful thinking on my part because her image provoked sexual yearnings.

Clandine noticed my fascination with the pixcube. She said, "That's Ozerta, a staff member of the Medical Complex, an overseer of the House of Rebirth. She makes life and death decisions. I suspect that she cooperates in covering up assassinations of those people who learn too much about the conspiracy. I see that her image has you entranced. You'll have to be very careful in contacting her. Don't let any of the sexual attraction you might feel for her interfere with our objectives."

Clandine paused.

I continued to look at the image of Ozerta.

"Aren't you going to ask me about your cover story for her, Rathe?"

"Oh, sure. What is it?"

"Tell her that you were reborn a blanc without the benefits of the House of Rebirth. Explain that you don't have a wristlock that identifies you. Ask her if there is any way she can help you. She lives near the Medical Complex but she may not be home. The rumors are that she uses All Hues Day to seek out prospective sexual partners of both sexes. I don't think you should approach her unless you can't find Flantel or Boget."

"Why is that?" I asked.

"Because she's dangerous, Rathe. She uses her sexual aura to entrap and confuse. I think you are way too vulnerable right now. If you can't find either of the other two rainbows, make certain that you spend some time with one or more holiday hedonists before seeking out Ozerta."

"Who and what are the holiday hedonists?"

"Those persons who practice sexual variety during any holiday. You can recognize them easily—they're the ones who appear nude in public."

Clandine's information made me realize how much I didn't know about this culture. I hoped I wasn't too ignorant to make an effective spy.

*   *   *

On All Hues Day, I finished my morning grooming, put on my freshly cleaned tunic, reviewed instructions and directions with Clandine, exited the building and entered the wildness and weirdness of the citywide celebration. As I took the slideways that would take me to the Color Wheel, I saw most people wore tunics but some were wearing costumes made out of strips of colored paper. A few were nude, the holiday hedonists that Clandine had told me about.

When I got off to change slidestrips a naked man offered me an orange paper hat. I took it, thanked him, put it on, and continued on my way, uninterested in what else he might be offering, and determined to carry out Clandine's plan. I had never seen the outside of the Color Wheel but I had no trouble recognizing it. It was the only building shaped like a large squat cylinder. I had returned to my rootless beginning.

I stifled the memories of my previous time here by mentally listing the improvements in my life since then: One: I was not in immediate danger of dying. Two: I had food, clothing, and shelter. Three: I liked what I knew about my new self. Four: I knew more about the culture. Five: I had prospects of a better life.

There were crowds around the various booths where white wristlock wearers were dispensing jarva, holiday food, paper hats, and rainbow imprinted paper streamers. The crowd noise hovered in the air like a melody line over the bass beat of drums. I went around the crowd toward Flantel's dwell, holding a drink of jarva punch in one hand and some rainbow-colored food cubes in the other. With both hands full, no more food and drink would be forced upon me by manic celebrants, whose high spirits seemed to mask a desperate hysteria just as their paper masks hid their features.

By the time I reached Flantel's building I'd drunk the punch and eaten the food cubes. I found no one home at his dwell. A nude woman in the corridor told me that most of the building's residents had gone to dance to the drums. I headed back toward the sound of the drums which reminded me of the autofactory section scene of drums where I'd followed Lyonella. What I had thought might be a meeting of the Freedom Crusaders had been a private rehearsal for the public celebration of a holiday.

I realized that my thinking had been strongly influenced by Clandine's suspicions, which might have no basis but a tendency on her part to paranoia. People clustered around the drums, some rocking to the beat, others dancing in their individual styles.

Flantel's height and blond hair helped me locate him. He was engrossed in watching one of the dancers. She was naked, her skin as black as a starless night sky. With her movements she created a unity with the drumming, shaking her rounded hips in what appeared to be joyous freedom. I kept edging closer until I was standing next to Flantel. His eyes never left the dancer.

I felt her eyes on me and I shifted my gaze from Flantel to her. Her hair lay almost flat against her skull in tight waves. Her eyebrows arched over large eyes as dark as her skin. A straight nose with rounded nostrils led my eyes to her lips, their fullness enhanced by a coating of purple paint, the same shade of purple as that of the food cubes. From the neck down she was hairless with nipples and labia painted purple.

I hadn't realized how hypnotic the dancer and the drums were until the drumming stopped. Flantel had been captivated too. He hadn't moved from his place beside me. If he had left I wouldn't have noticed. I realized that I was too easily distracted to make a good secret agent. Flantel stepped forward and reached out as if to take the dancer by the arm.

She looked at him and said, "Don't be a usurper. I want a purple slurper."

Flantel answered in the same rhyming style, "I feel passion's burn. What I don't know, I'll learn."

"If you come my way, you'll stay all day," she replied.

Flantel said, "I'll say goodbye to the pack in case I never come back."

The dancer took him by the hand and said, "Come to my place so I can sit on your face." They left. I tried to follow but lost sight of them when the drumming resumed and a cluster of people wearing orange hats like the one I still had on came between me and the pair I wanted to shadow.

By the time I convinced the orange hat group that I had places to go and things to do, Flantel and the dancer were nowhere to be seen. I handed the orange hat to the first hatless person I saw and walked toward the nearest slidestrip. Ahead of me on the walkway I saw a nude woman who, from the rear, looked like Lyonella. I caught up to her.

She turned to look at me with a smile.

She was someone I'd never seen before.

"Excuse me; I thought you were someone I knew."

She smiled and said, "I'm someone you can get to know easily."

"Thanks, but I better not. I was really looking for a particular person."

"I'm particular and I like the way you look. Come with me and we'll get acquainted in the old, familiar, intimate way."

It seemed like everyone was celebrating the holiday with sensual excess except me. I was committed to following Clandine's agenda as my main hope for getting a wristlock of my own. I said, "I appreciate the offer but I really approached you because I thought you were a friend of mine."

"I'm willing to be a new friend or we can go to some darkened nook and I'll pretend to be anyone you want and make you feel wanted. I play the Game every day but holidays. Today I'll play any game you want."

"The offer is appreciated but I'm committed to other plans." I hurried away before the temptation became too great to resist. I had to find Boget or Ozerta before the holiday ended.

TWELVE

Boget's dwell was near the Simulike Palace. Seeing that edifice brought back memories—the fascinating, dreamlike experience I'd had as a tribal initiate and the disturbing experience of being arrested by the Variation Investigation Service. I hoped to find Boget at home but I thought that learning something which would either justify or negate Clandine's suspicions seemed unlikely.

Boget answered the door, apparently surprised at the sight of an unexpected visitor. He scrutinized me before asking, "Are you sure you've come to the right dwell?"

"I have, if you are Boget."

I knew he was Boget but I didn't want to reveal that I had seen Clandine's pixcube of him. "My name is Rathe. I've come to you for advice."

He frowned. "Have you mistaken me for a Listener?"

"No. I've been to a Listener." I thought I should reveal that just in case there was some kind of conspiracy or association involving both Lyonella and Boget. "I came to you because you are the overseer of the Simulike Palace. Two people in the urbode where I used to dwell said that you were a rainbow who took an interest in grays, that you expanded the Simulike Palace facilities and made sure that all grays had access."

"It is my goal to ensure that the Simulike experience is available to all," he said.

"That's my problem. I was enjoying my first Simulike experience when I was arrested by the VIS. They are not following me now and I don't think they'll find my visiting you a suspicious act."

He continued looking at me with a puzzled expression, but not saying anything.

"May I come inside and tell you the details. I think you're my best hope for a solution to my problems."

Boget invited me in with some reluctance. I think the VIS arrest statement piqued his curiosity as I had hoped it would.

I had never been in a rainbow's dwell before. It was at least three times as spacious as Lyonella's dwell.

Boget, now playing the role of concerned host, offered me a seat and a drink of punch. I accepted both. The seat was comfortable; the punch tasted better than the holiday punch being served in the public places.

I told Boget about awakening as a nu-blanc in the Rainbow Room and escaping death by solving the equation and getting help from a gray.

Boget stopped my narration by asking, "You solved the equation?"

"Yes. If I had a wristlock of my own I could go back there and start my own advancement. But I'd rather play the Game. I tried it once and discovered that I'm good at it. I want your advice on how I can get a valid wristlock."

"What's wrong with the one you have? Is it a fake?"

"No. It belongs to someone the VIS wants to investigate for possible illegal activities."

"How did you get it?"

"From a rogue gray who helped me escape from the Color Wheel. He provided me with this wristlock as a favor to me, or so I thought. However, when I went to the Simulike Palace, my session was interrupted by the VIS who arrested me, thinking I was a suspected criminal."

"Was that just before the last Transit?"

"Yes, it was."

"So that was you… You actually escaped from the VIS? How?"

"I haven't really gotten away. One VIS officer took custody of me, hoping I can lead her to the gray whose wristlock I'm wearing. I don't have the resources to do that and I'm afraid when she realizes that I can't help her, she will send me to the Blanc Reeducation Center. I don't want to be reconditioned and brainwiped. It represents death to the person that I currently am."

"Rathe, you seem to be an unusually capable person, solving equations, showing Game skills, and, above all, surviving. Most blancs get reconditioned just a few shifts after they arrive. I see why the gray befriended you; he probably hoped to make use of your abilities. The VIS officer wants to use you, too. What has she promised you?"

"A wristlock, if all goes the way she wants it to, but I'm concerned that it won't work out and I'll lose my identity."

"I've noticed that you haven't given me any names. Why is that?"

"I don't want to be the cause of trouble for anyone who helps me."

"You're loyal in addition to being capable and talented. I may be able to help you if you're willing to wear a white wristlock and work in the Simulike Palace for a while."

"I could do that. I was fascinated by the Simulike experience."

"I have a new version of the Simulike machine here in one of the rooms. You can have a Simulike experience here if you want and you'll be in no danger of VIS interruptions—they've got their hands full with the holiday crowds. I'd like your feedback on whether or not you consider the new machine an improvement. I can't get much done today because of the holiday. If you are willing to stay here until tomorrow I can check on a few things and I may be able to help you."

There was no way for me to refuse the invitation without making Boget suspicious. I accepted.

He showed me to a room which contained a Simulike machine. "This model has a redesigned headband and no wristlock is required; the on button is centered on the headband. There is food and drink in the storage unit. The lav is on your right. I think that's everything you'll need today. In the morning I'll see what I can do about getting you a new wristlock. I have to leave now; I have a party to attend."

I thanked Boget and he left. I didn't know if I could trust him or not but I had no other choice than to stay and find out. With his help, I might get a wristlock and find myself free of Clandine and her conspiracy theories. But if Clandine was right in her suspicions, I was dealing with a conspirator who might want to prevent me from reporting anything to a VIS officer.

After some reflection, I decided not to worry about things I couldn't change and try the Simulike machine. The golden headband went on easily. I lay down, pressed the button—a curtain came down in my mind.

When it rose, I was one of a small group sitting on cushions before a tall, brown-skinned man with gray curly hair, dressed in a plain brown robe, who said, "I am the path guide. Are you here because you suspect there are pitfalls in the two common paths of convention and rebellion?"

Several people answered yes.

The path guide said, "All paths have their dangers. The major hazard on the conventional path is mindless conformity to standards and ideas that may be obsolete or flawed. The principal peril of the rebellious path is unthinking rejection of almost all that is customary and traditional without seeking satisfactory alternatives. Between these two extremes there are many paths suitable for individuals who are willing to examine their lives, think for themselves and take responsibility for their individual actions. Each of you will enter the evaluation chamber where the mind scanners will gather data on your past, your present and your potential future. You will then enter a counterfeit future based on your individual reality. What you learn there will help you find your own path."

The mind scanning was painless. I wondered if the technology would find the memories I had lost when I had been brainwiped, before I had become Rathe.

When my evaluation was finished I walked out of the evaluation chamber and into a projected future that seemed as real to me as yesterday. The setting was a wide walkway with tents on both sides.

I was walking along when I was hailed by a man dressed in fitted black and white clothes and wearing a tall black hat who was standing in front of a tent. "I am the Magician," he said. "I've got tricks, treats, and treasures. Sign on as my associate and I will explain everything to you. There's some of the magician in you. Share that part of you with me and I can give you the new ideas you need."

The Magician reminded me of Errox. He seemed capable but not quite trustworthy. An apparent movement in the tent caught my eye. I got a quick glimpse of a woman who might be Lyonella. She was wearing an abbreviated magician's assistant costume and around her neck there was a custodial collar. I rushed into the tent and found a two-dimensional picture of a woman. Her face was turned away. I couldn't tell whether or not it was Lyonella. A flickering light had led me to believe I had seen movement.

"It's all an illusion, just a game," said the Magician. "With my help you can be a major player. Give me your abilities, your energy, and your integrity—I can make you a winner."

When I looked back into the tent, it appeared to be furnished in elaborate splendor.

The Magician said, "Whatever you desire I can provide if you swear allegiance to me."

"I understand your offer. Perhaps I'll see you later." I was certain that he represented Errox, the first person I'd associated with in this world. My mind leaped to the conclusion that Lyonella was in the tent because I wanted to see her. I wondered if she was represented in two dimensions because she was missing something that would have made her more real or if I lacked a complete image of her in my mind.

My next stop along the midway was a tent covered with symbols that were unknown to me. Inside sat a short dark woman with an oval face and tall conical hat that ended in a point. She looked up from the book she was studying and said, "Your past has been erased and your future has not yet been written. You will be part of the great change that is to come if you pass through the chaos undiminished."

"Tell me about the chaos, so that I can deal with it as it comes."

She turned several pages in the book, put her finger on a passage and read, "The illusions of the present are decaying. The corruption of the world wardens escalates. The old ways were means to obscure the truth, but the truth will not be squelched. The great change is almost upon us and it behooves us to be ready—even if we are not completely sure where the boundaries are."

I thanked her for the information, mentally noting that she, like Clandine, seemed to think that there were ominous forces at work that must be challenged and defeated. I walked past her tent, wondering how much of this simulation was fantasy and how much reality.

I stopped at a bubbling fountain and drank some water, splashing some in my face in an effort to refresh myself for the next encounter. Next I came to an ornate, luxurious tent where a blonde woman and a black-haired man, both wearing purple robes, sat on decorated chairs. They appeared not to notice me and went on talking to each other.

She asked, "What good is power if you don't exploit it?"

"I don't mind your minor amusements as long as they don't threaten the plan," he replied. "I do think that your petty power plays tend to distract you from our main objectives."

"You mean your objectives. Although our interests are compatible they are not identical."

I listened for a few more minutes but learned very little. Their argument was circular with each more interested in proving the other at fault than in attempting to reach an agreement on anything. I backed away from their bickering.

The two people were evidently in positions of power which they squandered and misapplied because of their pettiness. I couldn't relate their images to anyone I'd met. Perhaps they were in my future. I hoped that whatever relationship I might have with them would be minimal since they both seemed egotistical, arrogant, and prone to ignorant action.

In backing away I stumbled over an almost overgrown path that led me through green foliage, across a footbridge and into the edge of a glen. I heard voices and then saw the people. I realized that I was witnessing an interrogation. A man with light hair and pink face, dressed in a multicolored robe, was being questioned by a team of plainly dressed men and women.

A woman with hair the color of rust asked, "There are thousands of gods and goddesses that people have created and believed in. Why are there none in the religion you have created?"

The pink-faced man replied, "No one can prove or disprove the existence of any deity. I was protecting my followers from faith in myths, legends and wishful thinking."

The woman countered with, "I think—and other members of this panel may agree with me—that you created another god-free religion because you wanted to be the supreme authority. Your explanation of protecting followers from faith conflicts with your endorsement of reincarnation. The evidence supporting reincarnation is largely anecdotal."

Sweating, the pink-faced man replied, "A belief in reincarnation is logical. Nature recycles everything. Why shouldn't someone accept the idea that the essence of life is neither created nor destroyed but used again and again? Besides, reincarnation fits in with the culture we were creating. It gave the people at the bottom of the social order hope that things would be better in the next life."

"You've confirmed our worst suspicions with your own words," the rust-haired woman replied. "Instead of helping people deal with their existence in the here and now, you had them invest their hopes in a religion structured to keep them content in a life of dubious quality. Is there anything you wish to say before the panel passes judgment?"

The pink-faced man said, "I did it for the preservation of the culture."

A man on the panel said, "In so doing you promoted the inequities of the culture to the detriment of your individual followers. I judge you guilty of spiritual chicanery."

The other member of the panel agreed. The rust-haired woman said to the pink-faced man, "There is a monastery where all the monks take a vow of silence and spend their time working in the fields or mediating quietly in their cells. You can spend the rest of your days there or you can visit the suicide booth and hope for reincarnation."

The pink-faced man was led away. He didn't look back at the panel members. I replayed the words of the trial in my mind to be sure of what I had heard. I had accepted reincarnation as a fact, but now I realized that there was no proof of it or of any of the teachings of True Faith Forever. I had believed something on the basis of someone else's alleged faith—now that belief seemed to be two logical steps away from any verifiable reality.

Maybe reincarnation was a fallacy. I wondered what percentage of the information I believed was wrong. Was this a major element of my future—finding confusion to replace illusion?

I wandered through the greenery, making my own path toward a small structure I could see. The small structure was an onion-shaped dwell made out of wood. Sitting on the deck in front of it were two people who hadn't noticed my approach. The woman had golden skin, almond eyes, black hair and an athletic figure. The man was darkly tanned with a widow's peak of dark-brown hair. As I got closer to them I felt a sense of peace and contentment that was new to me.

They greeted me as if I were a welcome guest and offered me a drink of water. I hadn't realized how thirsty I was. I wondered about the peace I felt and asked, "Is this clearing a special place that makes people feel good just to be in it?"

She answered, "It's not the place, it's us." He said, "You feel the power of the love we share."

"I like the feeling. I want something like you have for myself. How can I achieve it?"

"It takes two people willing to commit to a life together, two people who strive to treat each other well and deal with each other on a continuing, loving basis," she answered.

"Will I find this in my life?" I asked.

He replied, "You've already taken the first step—recognizing that you want it. There are no guarantees but you are now more apt to find and create it since you know what you're looking for."

She said, "I hope you will be as fortunate as we are."

I was startled by the sudden appearance of an androgynous person dressed in a long black robe. The face was translucent skin stretched tightly over a fleshless skull. The hair was sparse and transparent.

"Don't mind me," the apparition said, "I'm just passing through on my way to aid in the final change of those whose time is short."

"Who are you?"

The almost lipless mouth opened wide as the apparition said, "I am Death, a milestone in the existence of all. I represent change in all its aspects. You will all see me again eventually because the death rate is one hundred percent. Life feeds on death. Death is not the opposite of life; it is the opposite of birth, a marker of passage. I go now for an appointment with one who thinks I can be delayed indefinitely because he has position and power. All the colors of the rainbow cannot cancel the grayness I bring."

Death walked on. I asked the man and woman if they could confirm what Death said about the death rate being one hundred percent because I thought rainbows had eternal life. They directed me to the Sage for answers.

I found the Sage, a small man with bright dark eyes who reminded me of Kahalyton, at a bend in the path. I asked him, "Does Death speak the truth?"

"Yes. There is no reason for Death to lie."

"Can you help me understand?"

"Close your eyes and I'll give you a vision."

I closed my eyes. I saw someone wearing a rainbow wristlock, someone who looked familiar but not identifiable. As I watched the rainbow wristlock grew larger until it encompassed all that I knew existed. The rainbow turned upside down and took the world with it. I felt like I'd been picked up and dumped on my head.

I opened my eyes and found myself in Boget's dwell, still connected to the Simulike machine.

I felt weak. I got up and helped myself to food and drink. Boget had asked me to tell him about my experience with the new version of the Simulike machine. I went to the door but it wouldn't open. I was locked in. I lay back down. I had a lot to think about.

THIRTEEN

In the morning Boget unlocked the door to the room where I'd spent the night. He invited me to join him for first meal whenever I was ready. After my morning cleansing rituals, I sat down across from him, more interested in what he had to say than in the food.

Boget said, "I'd like to hear about your Simulike experience, if you're awake enough to recount it."

I was wide awake. I wanted to know if Boget was going to get me a wristlock but he wanted to hear about my Simulike adventure.

He was the host and the one with the power in this relationship. I played the good guest, swallowed the last of the food cube I was eating, took a long drink of water, and gave him a detailed summary of my Simulike encounters with others.

When I was done, he asked me, "Did the people you saw there remind you of specific people in your life?"

"Some did and some didn't. I got the feeling that the ones I didn't recognize are people I'll meet in the near future."

I didn't give him any names. If he was part of the conspiracy that Clandine believed existed, I didn't want to reveal anything that might lead him to believe I was working against him.

"Did any of the Simulike characters remind you of me?"

"No. It's possible one of them represented you and I just didn't make the connection." I wondered if he was looking for an ego boost or for information about the future. He might have been seeking some other information but I couldn't be sure what it might be. I would be willing to polish his ego a bit if that was what it took to get a new wristlock, but I didn't want to lie to him any more than necessary, especially when I couldn't be sure what he wanted to hear.

I wasn't certain exactly what was going on. It was possible that he had recorded my Simulike experience and was asking about it to see if I would give an honest account.

Boget said, "I think I'm going to play an important role in your life. If your Simulike journey didn't bring you into my orbit, two major possibilities exist. It could be that our relationship is going to go so smoothly that you don't need to be prepared for it or, at the other extreme; our association may be limited in ways that can't yet be foreseen. I think the first possibility is the more likely one.

"I want you to be my assistant at the Simulike Palace, if you are willing. All of the old Simulike machines are being replaced with new ones like the one you used. The work should be finished today. I'd like for you to be my eyes and ears."

I didn't know what that position might entail but I wasn't going to turn it down if a new wristlock was part of the package.

"I'd like to do that but not while wearing a wristlock that identifies me as a suspected criminal. I wouldn't be of much help to you if I had to worry continually about being arrested by the VIS."

I tried to express my desires in terms that implied our interests coincided. I watched his reaction to see if my point of view fit with his intentions.

Boget smiled. He reached into his waist pouch and withdrew a white wristlock. He said, "This is for you."

This was what I'd been waiting for but I felt letdown. I had expected something more official. Maybe the ceremony came when the wristlock change was made and recorded. Then I got it. Of course, Boget must have procured another illegal wristlock. I wondered what new entanglement I was letting myself in for. I knew Clandine would be pleased to learn that Boget was providing illegal wristlocks to bancs, but I wasn't convinced our interests were the same. Regardless, the new wristlock was an improvement over Errox's castoff.

"I appreciate the attention you've given to my problem, Boget. I'm eager to wear a white wristlock. Can the change be made this morning?"

"I've made the arrangements. We can leave now."

We left the urbode and got on the outbound slidestrip. When we reached the slideway I paid attention to the route, adding it to my mental map. Our journey stopped at a purple urbode that looked like all the others. I had expected an official building of some sort. We went into the urbode and on the fifth floor we approached a dwell. The door opened at Boget's request.

He introduced me to the occupant, Dreena, a short woman who was thickset without being fat.

She said to me, "I'm pleased to meet you, Rathe."

I knew I'd heard her name before, but couldn't remember where or when.

To Boget she said, "Your runner said you needed my services. How can I help?"

Boget gave Dreena the white wristlock. "Put this one on Rathe. Dispose of the gray one he's wearing and destroy it. It belongs to someone who's in trouble with the VIS."

Dreena's expression changed as if she had just learned something of importance. Then I recalled Clandine having told me that Dreena was one of two illegal smitties used by Errox. I couldn't understand why Boget was using an illegal smitty. I didn't understand why he wasn't doing this in some kind of official manner, but I wasn't going to ask. My focus was on getting Errox's gray wristlock off and the white wristlock on.

"I'll do a remote demolition on the gray wristlock," Dreena said.

Boget said, "Good," to her. Then he turned to me and asked, "Can you find your way back to my dwell?"

"Yes," I said. "On the way, I made a mental map of our route."

"Okay. Come back to my dwell when you're finished. Your new wristlock is keyed to open my door. Then we'll go to the House of Rebirth and get Ozerta—she's the rainbow overseer there—to get you officially registered as a white wristlock wearer."

"I'll be looking forward to that." Ozerta was one of Clandine's conspiracy suspects. If Boget could use an illegal smitty and get Ozerta to register the event as officially sanctioned, then he and Ozerta might be conspirators. Perhaps they were not as dangerous as Clandine seemed to think, but they were definitely involved in some illegal activity. Two rainbows who were bypassing the existing system.

I wondered why they were doing it. Maybe they were just going around the bureaucracy to save time and effort. Rainbows held the power in this society. Surely they could change the system if they wanted to? I wondered if Clandine had detected some irregularities and deduced a conspiracy, mistaking shortcuts for corruption.

Boget said goodbye to Dreena and left. She had me sit in a chair. Her setup was just like the one that Hushel had used to give me Errox's wristlock.

Dreena locked my right arm in the frame, fit the wires to my fingers, and removed the gray wristlock with the spreading tool. She wasn't as skilled as Hushel. She scraped my knuckles deep enough to make them bleed.

"I'm sorry. I'll put some antiseptic new skin on your knuckles." She picked up an unmarked container and sprayed on a liquid that stung me. Dreena removed the gray wristlock from the machine and said, "I'll get rid of this gray wristlock while the new skin dries."

She left before I could make a reply. I hoped she wouldn't be long. Although I was glad to be rid of Errox's wristlock, I felt vulnerable without a wristlock of my own. My wrist looked naked without one.

I looked around the dwell from my position in the chair where I was imprisoned by the hardware attached to my right arm. The dwell held nothing to distinguish it from other gray dwells except the smitty equipment.

After a while I began to wonder when Dreena would return. What if the VIS came to arrest her and took me, too? What if she was doing the wristlock demolition and injured herself? What if she never came back? I realized my thoughts were becoming paranoid and I started counting backwards from one hundred, one number with each breath, in an attempt to calm myself. I kept losing count as unpleasant thoughts flitted through my mind.

The way the hardware was attached to my right arm held me in place. I couldn't reach any of the controls with my left hand. The chair was firmly attached to the floor and wouldn't move despite my struggles. If Dreena never came back, would Boget look for me when I didn't return to his dwell? Was it possible that Boget suspected I was really an agent for Clandine and the VIS? If he did was he intending to have me killed or brainwiped?

I shuddered at the idea of being brainwiped again. Regardless of who I had been before, I was now Rathe. I had a character and a personality that I could live with. I hoped I hadn't fallen into a trap that meant I would have to start over as a blanc or a rebirth.

My hopes were at low ebb when Dreena finally returned. She wasn't alone. Alongside her was Errox.

"Rathe, my friend, I'm glad to see you again."

"Hello, Errox." I saw that he was wearing a green wristlock, probably the one he'd cut off the dead woman in the Rainbow Room. I tried to banish the memory from my mind.

Errox looked at Dreena and ordered, "Install his white wristlock, Dreena. Rathe is on his way up in the world." Then turning to me he said, "When you figured out the color tile pattern in the Rainbow Room I knew you had the potential to be somebody valuable."

"I'm making my way as best I can," I said, wondering what he meant by 'valuable.' Valuable to him, most certainly, but how? I had seen the way Errox treated the grays and those he believed were beneath him. I didn't want to be included in his entourage.

Dreena compressed my hand with her machine and slipped the white wristlock onto my wrist. She said, "Your hand will hurt for several shifts."

She handed me some pills in a clear plastic tube. "Take one of these for the pain. No more than two per shift."

"Rathe is experienced. He's been through this before."

Turning to me, Errox said, "The problem you had last time was unexpected. I never meant for you to fall into the hands of the VIS."

"I didn't think you helped me just so I could be arrested," I replied.

"How did you manage to get released?"

"One of the VIS agents wanted to use me as an information source. I don't trust the VIS. I went to Boget to find a way out."

I didn't think I was telling Errox anything he didn't know. Since Dreena had sought out Errox and brought him back here, I could reasonably assume that she had told him everything she knew about me and Boget.

"Hear that, Dreena? Rathe hasn't been around for two transits yet and he's already slidestrip smart and walkway wise."

Dreena nodded yes as she finished cleaning the blood off her equipment, the dried blood from my knuckles that she'd scraped getting the gray wristlock off my wrist. I was certain the scraping had been no accident, just a ploy to give her a chance to leave me here and contact Errox. Since she knew how to find him, he must trust her or need her. She didn't have the subservient attitude toward Errox that Ural and Miral had shown in their dealings with him.

He looked at me knowingly. "When I gave you my wristlock, I thought you'd eventually go back to the Rainbow Room and upgrade your wristlock color by beating the odds and getting into the winner's circle."

"I was considering that as a possibility, but I was arrested before I had a chance to follow through." I had thought about it. I knew the danger would be minimal if the equation stayed the same. But if the Rainbow Room equation was different, or if it changed while I was there, I could lose my life if I didn't figure out the new equation. My main plan had been to find a way I could play the game. I knew I was good at that. In addition to the danger in the Rainbow Room, I was reluctant to return to the scene of the most traumatic experience of my present life.

"Your VIS arrest would have never happened if Boget and Wanklurm hadn't disagreed."

I asked, "Who is Wanklurm?"

"He's the rainbow who is Chief of the VIS. He and Boget argued over how things should be done so Wanklurm decided to have me arrested to prevent my helping Boget."

"You're helping Boget?"

"I'm one of his most important associates. Have you heard about the new Simulike machines?"

"Yes. I had a Simulike experience in the one in Boget's dwell."

"What did you think of it as compared to the experience in the Simulike Palace before the VIS interruption?" he asked.

"My first experience in the Palace was engrossing. At the time I was struggling to find my own identity. The Simulike experience was like living another person's life as his own identity was confirmed. In the second experience, the one in Boget's dwell, I was myself in a series of encounters with other characters, some from my present, some possibly in my future. The second experience was more meaningful and seemed that it might be useful as my life unfolds by making me aware of whom I'd be dealing with."

Errox's expression became guarded, a change from the open-faced, nothing-to-hide look that he'd been wearing since he entered Dreena's dwell. He asked, "Was I represented in the experience?"

"Yes, you were a magician who told me I could become a winner, a major player."

He smiled. "You can, Rathe, with my guidance."

"I've got to get registered before I can play the Game."

"Not that Game. It's a diversion, useful in several ways, but it's not the game that matters to winners like you and I."

"I'm not sure what you mean."

"You will later. Now that you've got your wristlock, you're going back to Boget's dwell, aren't you?"

Since I was reasonably certain that Dreena had told Errox I was going back to Boget's dwell, I answered in the affirmative. "He's going to get me registered as a white wristlock wearer."

"I'll come along with you. I want to tell Boget that the installation of the new machines at the Simulike Palace has been completed."

I didn't have much trust in Errox's friendliness, but I had no reasonable way to decline his company. If he was truthful in his statements about being a valuable associate of Boget's, I might be having more dealings with him.

My Simulike experience had indicated that I shouldn't trust the magician. I wasn't sure I could trust Boget either. He had gotten me the promised wristlock but his association with both Dreena and Errox made me somewhat suspicious of his methods and ethics. Of course, I hadn't met anyone yet that I had complete trust in, except perhaps Kahalyton and he had his own agenda. Maybe I could trust Lyonella when she wasn't under the influence of Cainenol.

Errox kissed Dreena goodbye just before we left to go to Boget's dwell. That confirmed one of my suspicions, but I kept that suspicion and all the others to myself for now.

FOURTEEN

On the slideway Errox and I made our way toward Boget's dwell. Errox seemed more relaxed than he had been at our previous meetings. Before he had been competent with a somewhat forbidding manner, a facade of confidence and arrogance that discouraged or deflected questions. Now he seemed much more open and friendly, as if things were going his way. The difference in his mood was his happiness.

Why shouldn't Errox be happy? He had a green wristlock, probably had Dreena as a lover, and also had a working relationship with Boget. Although Errox's manner suggested that he might now answer the kinds of questions that he would have rebuffed before, I didn't ask any because I wasn't sure I could trust his answers.

If Clandine's conspiracy theory had a factual basis, Boget might have brought Errox into his schemes for some illegal purpose. I believed Errox was an unlikely choice of an associate for Boget unless Boget was attempting to rehabilitate him. Maybe Boget was helping Errox just as he was helping me. I couldn't be certain of that, but I would probably learn more about their relationship when we reached Boget's dwell. I decided my best path for now was to maintain comfortable relationships with both

Errox and Boget until I discovered more about the nature of their association.

I needed more information but I wasn't going to ask any unsettling questions until I was registered in the House of Rebirth as a bona fide wearer of a white wristlock. Once I had that legitimacy, I would be in a better position to make decisions about my immediate future. I had accomplished one of the things that Clandine wanted me to do. I had located Errox. But I wasn't going to tell that to Clandine yet, not until I knew more about the situation.

Errox had saved my life and I didn't want to betray him. Regardless of what motivated him to help me, he had enabled me to continue living. I owed him for that.

Previously, Clandine had led me to believe that finding Errox would allow him to end his troubles with the VIS. I wasn't sure that was true, now. Clandine's power was limited compared to that of Boget. Boget might be able to do more for Errox than Clandine could ever do. I needed to find out if there actually was a conspiracy before making any potentially rash decisions. If there was a conspiracy, I wanted to discover whether it had sinister implications or was merely an agreement among certain rainbows to bypass unwieldy procedures.

Both Errox and I became aware of mass movement on the slidestrips ahead of us. Most of the people moved over to the slowest strip to get off. I could see a crowd had gathered in front of one of the urbodes. Errox said, "Let's see what's happening."

We moved over to the slowest strip and got off at the urbode's apron. A crowd gathered around the cluster of VIS who encircled the urbode. As we watched, the VIS brought the urbode residents out in a single file, all of them wearing custodial collars and chained together. I felt a constriction in my own neck, remembering when I had been collared. I wondered what deviation these grays were being accused of.

Errox stared as if transfixed. The tightness of his face showed an extreme emotional reaction—anger, maybe rage, and other emotions that I couldn't identify. Instead of asking him anything I listened to the people in the crowd.

"What are they doing?" asked a young woman, addressing her question to whomever might answer.

An older man with a resigned expression said, "That's Chief Wanklurm's elite squad. They're arresting all the grays in that urbode."

Someone else in the crowd, someone I couldn't see clearly said, "They're all Freedom Crusaders. They refused to move on Transit Day. They breached the portal plate and declared the urbode a safe house for anyone seeking freedom. I knew it wouldn't work. You can't fight the VIS."

The young woman who had asked what was happening broke free from the crowd. She ran toward the VIS officer who appeared to be in charge. His back was toward her. She leaped on him. With her right arm around his neck in a stranglehold, she yanked on her gray wristlock with her left hand. It exploded, killing her and the VIS officer, taking his head off. Gore splattered over the apron and I felt sick to my stomach.

What Hushel had told me was true—when you pull real hard on a wristlock it explodes and it renders bodies into chunks the size of food cubes. I was still stunned by what I had seen when Errox tapped me on the shoulder and gestured toward the center of the slideway.

We quickly got back on the center slidestrip and proceeded to the urbode where Boget lived. Neither of us spoke. It was as if our silence was some sort of homage paid to the deaths we had just witnessed.

We went to Boget's dwell and, as promised, my new wristlock opened the door.

Boget was surprised that Errox was with me. If he was disconcerted, he covered it well by playing the good host, inviting us to sit down and offering us a drink of hot cokafa. Errox and I both accepted the offer. Boget made preparations for the brew and set a timer to ring when the drink was hot.

Errox said, "I came by to tell you that the new Simulike machines are all in place and the Palace can be reopened."

"That's good, Errox. Ahead of schedule."

Turning to me, Boget said, "Rathe, I want you to become familiar with all aspects of the Simulike Palace so that you can report to me the patrons reactions to the new machines. I believe that the data generated by the Simulike experiences can be used for the common good—"

The bell indicating the cokafa was hot interrupted Boget.

Errox said, "I'll get the drinks."

Boget continued telling me about the possibilities of Simulike data.

Errox came back with three cups and sat them down on the table. I was surprised that Errox served us. It didn't seem in keeping with his usual behavior. Perhaps the death scene had affected him strongly. We all sipped the hot, brown beverage.

When Boget paused between sips, Errox said to him, "You could spend more time with the Simulike data if I took over greater responsibility in our projects."

"Errox, I believe that your ambition knows no limits."

Errox, flashing a smile that was probably intended to be disarming, said, "Of course I'm ambitious. That's one of the reasons you chose me as an associate. But I'm also concerned about you. You haven't had your usual level of high energy lately. I thought that with the new Simulike machine installation complete and with Rathe joining the Simulike Palace crew, you could let me handle things. Now you could take some time off. Rathe could be running the entire Palace in a cycle or two and I could take care of our other enterprises."

Boget shrugged.

I said, "I'm a fast learner and a willing worker."

Boget said to Errox, "I don't think this is the right occasion to discuss this."

When he said the word occasion he shifted his focus from Errox to me for an instant. I perceived that he was indicating to Errox that he didn't want to talk about their other projects while I was present. I didn't volunteer to leave, not only because I had no particular place to go but mainly because I wanted to learn more about their activities.

Boget took a deep drink of his cokafa, draining the cup. I did the same. Errox had only taken one small sip of his.

Errox looked at our empty cups, glanced at me, and then said to Boget, "You and I both recognize the potential that Rathe has. A short time ago he was a nu-blanc that someone had dumped in the Rainbow Room. He figured out how to get out alive. Then he didn't have a wristlock, didn't know his name or the name of anyone else. Now he's got a white wristlock and he's sitting in the dwell of one of the most powerful people on the planet. He's more than just a survivor—he's a high achiever. He's going to figure everything out. I think he should be told what's going on."

"Errox, that isn't your decision to make." Boget's speech was slightly slurred and he seemed to be having trouble focusing his eyes. I wondered if he really was overtired or in bad health.

"Rathe already knows that you deal in unauthorized wristlocks because you provided one for him. He didn't go running to the VIS to report you. He understands that sometimes you have to make your own way as best you can. Right, Rathe?"

I couldn't deny that. I started to speak but my tongue seemed strangely thick. I nodded. I realized that I felt peculiar, like the cokafa had upset my system.

Boget looked at me, saw that I wasn't feeling well, and asked Errox, "Did you poison the cokafa?"

"No, I just added a little something that a friend borrowed from the medical center. It's a drug used to quiet belligerent patients physically and mentally. Your body will become too relaxed to move and your mental attitude will be cooperative."

Errox turned to me and said, "I had to dose you too, Rathe, to keep you from interfering."

I wasn't able to move my arms or legs. I couldn't take any action, even if I'd wanted to.

Errox said to Boget, "I want a rainbow wristlock. I've heard that you have one, ready for the next lover who meets all your needs. Where is it?"

Boget seemed to have no resistance. He said, "In the drawer underneath my sleep platform. Errox went to the drawer, opened it, and removed the rainbow wristlock. He turned it over and over in his hand, admiring it. Then he put it in his waist pouch and came back to the table.

Ignoring me, he said to Boget, "When I get Dreena to put this on me, I'll be able to open the storage locker in the Simulike Palace where the Cainenol is kept. I'm going to take over the trade, Boget. You will be the silent partner. Where's the rest of the Cainenol?"

"It's all in the storage locker."

"How do you get more?"

"It comes to the transporter station in the House of Rebirth with each new shipment of human blancs from the other worlds."

I was startled by the information I was getting. We were not alone. There were other worlds and there was contact between worlds. As soon as that information registered in my mind, I wondered why blancs were sent here from those other worlds. Was the House of Rebirth no more than a receiving station for blancs from elsewhere?

The implications were staggering. I had been told that reincarnation was the process by which humans began new lives with new bodies, that everyone was reincarnated, but only rainbows retained their memories. How much of what I had been told was true? Was I in a culture full of disinformation?

I heard Errox ask Boget, "When is the next shipment due?"

Boget, whose speech was slurred by the drugged cokafa, answered, "Ozerta knows. I don't. There've been some problems." His voice trailed off.

"What problems?" Errox demanded.

Boget's head lolled. Drool dripped from his mouth onto his tunic.

Errox shook him and repeated, "What problems?"

Boget blinked his eyes, looked at Errox and said, "At the Outpost, the Cainenol is packed into the pods with the nu-blancs. Sometimes the nu-blancs escape when the pods are opened and the Cainenol is illegally unloaded. The pods are not supposed to be discharged until they arrive at the rebirthing room in the House of Rebirth. The overseers at the Outpost have reported the blanc problem."

"What's Ozerta doing about it?"

Boget seemed to have fallen asleep. Errox slapped him in the face and repeated his question when Boget's eyes opened.

Boget mumbled, "She's in the Fane of Change getting the rejuv treatments. She should be out today."

Errox made a sound of disgust and said, "You people are too soft. You need me to put some spine into the organization. Ozerta is too vain, getting rejuv treatments when she should be taking care of business. Flantel has never put out enough effort. Wanklurm runs roughshod over all of you. I'm going to take his place. I'm going to run this show and you're going to be a silent partner. Do you hear me?"

I was making sense of some, but not all, of what I heard. Clandine's conspiracy theories seemed to be true. Her suspects, Boget, Flantel, and Ozerta, were part of a conspiracy to distribute Cainenol and provide illegal wristlocks. Clandine hadn't mentioned anything about Wanklurm. Errox had told me that Wanklurm was the rainbow who was chief of the VIS. I wondered if Clandine suspected him. She might have suspected him, but has been unwilling to tell me. Clandine evidently hadn't known how deeply Errox was involved in the Cainenol smuggling. I was trying to put everything together, but I still didn't have all the pieces of this puzzle.

Errox seemed to have worked himself into a rage. In a loud voice he said to Boget, "Get used to it. Wanklurm is history. I'm going to eliminate him."

Feeling very groggy, I tried to figure out how a person who was immortal could be eliminated. No answer was forthcoming in my fuzzy head. Boget mumbled something about warning Wanklurm. Suddenly, everything went black and I felt myself falling....

FIFTEEN

"Wake up. Wake up."

I heard the voice and, for a moment, thought that I was back in the Rainbow Room. I tried to focus my eyes, to get ready to move over the treacherous tiles before they collapsed. What I saw were two large men, with rainbow wristlocks, both of them strangers to me. One of them, a blond with blue eyes that glared at me, stepped forward as if to grab me by the shoulders and shake me.

The other one, the brown-haired one, put a restraining hand on his shoulder as he said, "Take it easy, Incate. Let's find out what's going on first."

He then looked at me. I was surprised to see that his right eye was brown and his left eye green. He said to me, "My name is Prevance. My partner's name is Incate. We came to see Boget but it looks like we're too late."

Incate asked, "Why did you kill Boget?"

"I didn't. He was alive when I passed out."

"Well," Incate said, "someone broke his neck. If it wasn't you, who was it?"

Prevance made a stop gesture with his right hand to Incate, and then tuned to me asking, "Who are you? Why are you here and what happened to Boget?"

"My name is Rathe," I replied, trying to keep from snapping back. "Boget offered me the opportunity to assist in the operation of the Simulike Palace. One of Boget's associates, a man named Errox, was also here. He drugged the cokafa that Boget and I drank. He wanted information from Boget. He got frustrated with the answers he was getting and became enraged. After that, I don't know what happened. You'll have to ask him."

Incate said, "I don't believe you. I think you're part of one of Boget's illegal schemes. I also believe you killed him. I don't see any cups, any cokafa, or any other evidence of anyone named Errox."

"Take it easy, Incate. I'm sure Rathe is eager to cooperate."

Then facing me, Prevance said, "We're special investigators, here to check into Boget's activities. We found you with a dead body. We are determined to uncover exactly what happened. Is there anyone who can support your story?"

The answer came to me immediately. "Boget can tell you himself. All you have to do is send his body to the Fane of Change and have him reincarnated. Then, he'll be able to tell you what actually happened."

Incate emitted a grunt of disgust. "Rathe, you can't possibly be that naive. You wouldn't be here in Boget's dwell if you were ignorant about his activities."

"I don't understand what's going on. Boget's a rainbow: reincarnate him and let him tell you who his murderer was. Or is there some reason you don't want Boget brought back to life?"

Prevance answered, shaking his head in disbelief. "There is no way Boget's mind and body can be reanimated. He's dead, and he's not coming back to life. Incate thinks you know that. I don't know what you know. Why don't you tell me what's going on in your head?"

I looked Prevance in the eyes, first the brown one and then the green one. I found the contrast between eyes oddly upsetting, but not as disturbing as Incate's hostility. "According to what I've been told, rainbows are immortal. When they die, they go to the Fane of Change and they are reincarnated in the same body. The body is rejuvenated and they retain all their memories. Are you telling me that there is some reason Boget can't be reincarnated? Something I don't know or haven't been told?"

Incate moved closer to me in an intimidating manner, "I can't believe you're taking that lame line with us. Nobody has solid proof that anybody has ever reincarnated. Everybody knows that."

Prevance held a hand up to silence Incate. Then he said to me, "My partner is a confirmed skeptic. I'm open-minded. Although reincarnation can't be proved, it can't be disproved either. Either way, the Fane of Change has nothing to do with it. That's just the place where rainbows go for rejuvenation treatments."

Incate gave a disapproving look to Prevance, "We're here to get information, not to give it. Let's take Rathe back to the overseer's center and have a vericator session with Nordel and Yondoka."

I didn't know who Nordel and Yondoka were. I was shocked by what I had learned. Rainbows were not immortals according to Prevance and Incate. Errox had indicated that the alleged reincarnated beings that emerged from the House of Rebirth were not reincarnations of the people of this world but were blancs that had been sent here from other worlds, other worlds I hadn't known existed. There was a lot I didn't know and I was learning all the time that much of what I thought I knew was wrong.

"Let me tell you my story now so you can verify it later."

Incate started to object but Prevance silenced him with a hand gesture. "Go ahead, Rathe, tell us."

I told them the whole story. First about waking up in the Rainbow Room, not knowing who I was or where I was. I told them about the woman who died and how Errox had removed her green wristlock. Both of them seemed impressed when I told them about solving the equation that determined which tiles would collapse. I told them about Errox saving me from drowning, finding me places to stay, and having a smitty put Errox's gray wristlock on my wrist.

I recounted my arrest in the Simulike Palace by the VIS who thought I was Errox and the attack on the VIS station by the Freedom Crusaders.

Incate asked, "Who are these Freedom Crusaders?"

I told him the little I knew.

Prevance asked, "Then Errox is an important person in the Freedom Crusaders?"

"It seems so. At least he was important to the woman who died. She helped stage the raid on the VIS station to rescue him. She didn't know I was wearing his wristlock and that the VIS thought I was Errox."

"Why did the VIS let you go?"

I told them about Clandine and her plan to use me to locate Errox, to investigate the conspiracy, and help end the Cainenol problem. Prevance looked like he believed what I was saying.

Incate asked who Clandine suspected. I felt the complete truth was the only course of action open to me since I was going to be questioned while hooked to a vericator. I told them that Clandine had suspected Boget, Flantel, and Ozerta.

Incate, seeming more interested than hostile, asked, "No one else?"

"She suspected Errox was involved in some way. She also suspected a Listener named Lyonella, but I've met Lyonella and I think she's innocent. I don't know if Clandine still suspects her or not."

"Tell me why Errox drugged Boget?" Prevance asked.

"Errox wanted to take over the Cainenol operation. He wants to replace VIS Chief Wanklurm as head of the conspiracy."

Incate's jaw dropped. "Are you telling us that Chief Wanklurm is behind this conspiracy?"

"Yes, according to what Errox and Boget said."

Prevance inquired, "The VIS officer, Clandine, did she suspect Wanklurm?"

"If she did, she didn't tell me."

Prevance said, "So according to this conversation you heard between the drugged Boget and Errox, they were involved in a conspiracy to distribute Cainenol, with co-conspirators Flantel, Ozerta, and Wanklurm. What else were they doing?"

"I don't know about the others, but Boget was dealing with unauthorized wristlocks. He got this white one for me. Errox stole a rainbow wristlock that Boget had in the dwell."

Incate said, "It's time for a vericator session. Let's go to the overseers' urbode. Rathe, I'm going to have a stunner trained on you all the time we're on the slidestrips. If you do anything to make me use it, you won't enjoy the experience."

I didn't bother making a reply. I just got up and left with them. The slidestrip trip was uneventful. The only unusual thing I noticed was the increased number of VIS personnel patrolling everywhere, alert for any sign of trouble.

Inside the overseers' urbode, Prevance and Incate took me to what appeared to be a command center for their investigation. Incate watched me while Prevance sent one runner to get Nordel and Yondoka, another runner to notify the medical center personnel to pick up Boget's body and a third runner to notify Clandine that she was wanted in the overseers' urbode.

Incate left and returned with two rainbows. Prevance introduced them to me as Nordel and Yondoka. I immediately recognized them as the loving couple I had encountered in my recent Simulike experience. Nordel's handsome, tanned face showed lines of worry or concern. Yondoka's almond eyes were puffy with reddened lids that still held the hint of tears. I wondered what had caused the tears.

Prevance said to them, "Rathe was in Boget's dwell when Incate and I went to question Boget. Boget was murdered. According to Rathe, Boget was killed by a man named Errox. Do either of you know of Errox?"

Neither of them had heard of Errox.

Prevance resumed speaking. "Rathe has quite a story to tell. It involves a conspiracy, illegal wristlocks, Cainenol and a VIS officer named Clandine. We're waiting for her to arrive before using the vericator. Do you know Clandine?"

Yondoka spoke first. "Yes, I know Clandine. She's trying to stop the spread of Cainenol."

Nordel added, "I doubt if she's involved in any conspiracy. She sought us out as allies in her quest for the source of Cainenol. Her suspicions supported the evidence of corruption that we reported in the last batch of Delphic data we sent to the Council. So her suspicions are part of the reason that you and Incate are here to investigate the situation."

"I want her story verified before we tell her anything," Incate said. "She works for Chief Wanklurm and could be part of the conspiracy."

Prevance added, "My partner's suspicions are justified. None of us want to end up like Boget or your friend Jonter."

I was hearing information that was new to me. I didn't know anything about Delphic data and I had never heard of Jonter. Curiosity got the best of me. I asked, "Who is Jonter?"

Yondoka answered. "Jonter and Nordel and I all attained rainbow status recently. Jonter became aware that new rainbows were put in positions where they couldn't threaten the power structure of old rainbows. He thought that corruption was widespread and suspected that our culture was an artificial construct based on deceit and fallacies. He was about to go public with his information just before he was killed."

That explained Yondoka's tears. She had lost a friend.

Nordel put a comforting arm around Yondoka, as he said, "That's when we discovered that we were not immortals. The Fane of Change is a fraud. Rainbows die like everyone else. They just get a higher level of medical care and rejuvenation treatments that increase their life expectancy. Wanklurm reported that Jonter's killer was a berserker. We think that some of Wanklurm's elite guards are assassins who kill anyone Wanklurm considers a threat to his power."

"Let's stop telling everything we know to Rathe," interjected Incate. "He's still a murder suspect until his story is verified."

I was having problems absorbing all the disturbing information I was hearing. I felt faint.

Prevance looked at me, saw my condition and said, "Rathe, I think you need to rest before the vericator session. I'll take you to a sleep room and have a medic examine you to learn what you were drugged with."

As Prevance led me away. I heard Incate say to Nordel and Yondoka, "I'm not sure he was drugged. He knows too much. If he fails the vericator session, he's going to have to be brainwiped."

I was already half asleep when the medic came. She told Prevance that my blood work showed signs of having been drugged. I was relieved that a portion of my story had been verified. When she left I went to sleep.

Prevance awakened me gently, saying, "Clandine is here. Her vericator session confirms that she was using you as an undercover agent. Now it's time for you to tell your story while connected to the vericator."

I told the complete truth to the extent that I knew it. My story was verified. I felt as if the better part of the weight of the world had been taken off my shoulders. Even Incate acknowledged that most of my story fit with everything else they'd learned. When Prevance led me back into the command center conference room, there were four other people there—Nordel, Yondoka, Incate, and Clandine.

Nordel spoke first. "I want to thank Clandine and Rathe for their efforts and their cooperation. Now it's time for us to make plans to bring an end to the conspiracies around here."

"Rathe and Clandine shouldn't be here," Incate said. "Only rainbows should handle this problem."

Nordel replied in a stern voice, "We need all the help we can get. You and Prevance can't handle a problem of this magnitude alone. We need to keep track of the conspirators until we are sure we can neutralize them. We are going to need VIS personnel for that. Clandine is our only VIS contact so far. Clandine, are there other VIS personnel we can trust?"

Clandine replied that most of the VIS personnel were reliable, that she and her colleague Arvon had administered stress measuring tests to VIS officers who were all working extra shifts to cope with berserkers and Crusaders. The stress measuring tests also included, unbeknown to those taking the tests, questions that would reveal any allegiance to Wanklurm that overshadowed the VIS code of conduct. A concealed vericator had validated the results.

She said that so far it looked as if the only VIS personnel willing to follow Wanklurm blindly were the members of the elite guard.

Incate said, "All right. We need Clandine. Why do we need Rathe?"

Clandine answered, "Rathe is the only one of us who can identify Errox by sight. He found Errox when no one else could. He is an eyewitness that Errox is a murderer and a wristlock thief. He heard Boget admit to being a key player in the conspiracy. He knows where Dreena lives. He has done marvelous undercover work for me. We need him."

Incate opened his mouth as if to refute Clandine, but no words came out.

Nordel said, "The first thing we should do is arrest Dreena. We're probably too late to prevent her from putting a rainbow wristlock on Errox. If he's already got it, he has access to the current Cainenol supply. We may be able to get Dreena to tell us where he is and what he plans to do. Clandine, can you find someone to locate Dreena and arrest her?"

Nordel was taking charge. Incate looked frustrated. Prevance kept a neutral look on his face.

Clandine answered, "I'll get the directions from Rathe. I'll have Arvon send a squad over to arrest her and anyone else in her dwell."

Nordel said, "After second meal, I want all of us to meet back here. Yondoka and I will bring the rest of the rainbows that we are certain are trustworthy. Clandine, I'd like for you to invite all the loyal VIS personnel that can attend a meeting here without arousing Wanklurm's suspicions."

"Wanklurm is trying to hold down the civil unrest using mostly his elite guards. I shouldn't have trouble getting the rest of the VIS to come."

"Will this be a strategy meeting?" Prevance asked.

Nordel answered, "It's going to be more than that. When I sent in the report that brought you and Incate to help investigate, I didn't know as much about the misinformation we've all been exposed to. I intend to share this knowledge with all who attend the meeting. This conspiracy involves the very foundations of the culture we're living in. We've got to form the broadest alliance possible to combat the conspirators."

"You don't have the permission of the Council to reveal the secrets of the rainbows," Incate said.

"I don't need anyone's permission to tell the truth, not now, and not at any time in the future," was Nordel's reply.

I looked forward to the meeting. There was a lot I wanted to know and I believed that Nordel would tell me.

SIXTEEN

The meeting began after several more rainbows and a number of select VIS personnel had gathered in the overseers' urbode. Yondoka and Nordel took charge.

Yondoka spoke first. "As some of you know, Nordel and I started a group called the Alliance for Cultural Transformation. The purpose was to eliminate the deception and disinformation that is present in our daily lives. One of our techniques was to spread folk tales that contained elements of truth that were not common knowledge.

"We also shared information that conflicted with what we were conditioned to believe because our best predictive efforts indicated that our culture was decaying. Recent developments—the Cainenol problem, the appearance of blancs, the Freedom Crusaders, the practices of Wanklurm's elite guards, the disappearance or death of new rainbows who were disillusioned when they learned that they were not immortal—everything clearly shows that the entire system is corrupt, based on keeping the majority deceived."

Several people gasped. Evidently they were hearing for the first time that rainbows were subject to death. I understood the shock they felt since I'd been jolted by that information earlier.

"The rumor that we are in touch with other worlds is true. When the members of the Alliance for Cultural Transformation were unable to stop the Cainenol traffic, we asked for help from the Universalist Council, the governing body for the twenty-three known human worlds."

An ebony skinned VIS officer asked, "Are you telling us that there are twenty-two other worlds like this one?"

Nordel answered the question, "Yes. We don't have much information about them but we have determined that their cultures differ from ours."

There was a minute of silence as people absorbed that information.

"The Universalist Council assigned the problem to two rainbow investigators," Yondoka said. "They have stopped the traffic. No more Cainenol will reach our world, but the last shipment hasn't been distributed yet. We have a crew searching for it in the Simulike Palace where it has been stored. The two investigators are here to help us end the Cainenol problem. Incate and Prevance please stand so everyone here will know who you are and aid you as best they can."

Incate and Prevance stood up and received applause. Both seemed pleased by the recognition, but I suspected that inside they were unhappy not to be in charge. I was glad that Yondoka and Nordel were running this operation. They radiated competence and caring. I had reservations about Incate, who seemed hostile and impulsive, and Prevance, whose surface affability might be no more than a clever facade capable of disarming those who accepted him at face value.

"Part of the credit for uncovering the Cainenol conspiracy goes to VIS officer Clandine and her associate Rathe. Would the two of you stand up please?"

We stood up and received applause. I had never been applauded before. A warm glow seemed to fill my being, the best feeling I'd experienced since my most recent time with Lyonella.

"Boget, the overseer of the Simulike Palace," Yondoka continued, "was evidently the power behind the introduction of Cainenol. He is dead, killed by a man named Errox who wants to take over Boget's role. We have VIS personnel looking for Errox and the rainbows involved in this conspiracy."

A woman with an oval face and red hair asked, "Who are the other rainbow conspirators?"

"Ozerta, overseer of the House of Rebirth; Flantel, overseer of the Clerics Guild; and Wanklurm, chief of the VIS."

I heard sounds of surprise.

The red-haired woman asked, "What's being done about them?"

Yondoka answered, "We're not ready to do anything about Wanklurm, yet. He and his elite guards are occupied with the problem of the Freedom Crusaders. We intend to depose Wanklurm but a formal plan hasn't been developed yet. Flantel is a minor figure; we have him under surveillance. We don't know where Ozerta is but she doesn't represent a threat now that we've stopped Cainenol shipments to the House of Rebirth. She just completed rejuvenation treatments at the Fane of Change and left to visit friends. We have people looking for her."

A tall, handsome rainbow said, "When Ozerta comes out of the Fane of Change, she usually goes to see old lovers so they can appreciate her renewal." He sounded like the voice of experience.

"I think now is the time for Nordel to tell you what the Game really is," Yondoka said.

I remembered Lyonella telling me that the Game was not what it seemed. Getting confirmation of what she had told me gave me a feeling of greater warmth for her as well as a corresponding increase of trust in what she said and did. I listened intently as Nordel began to speak.

"The Game is a very sophisticated way of forecasting future probabilities. The mathematical foundation is a series of evolutionary techniques known as Delphi methods. These methods structure a group communication process that allows a group of individuals, as a whole, to deal effectively with one or more complex problems or situations."

That information seemed almost familiar to me, like something in a corner of my mind that I hadn't examined for a while.

Nordel continued. "The data generated by the Delphi method is fed into computers that have Bayesian networks. These networks are self-updating complex diagrams that organize data pertaining to a particular area by mapping out cause-and-effect relationships among important variables and encoding the variables with numbers that represent the probabilities of any one variable affecting any other variable. Such networks provide useful forecasting even when key bits of data are unavailable. The

Universalist Council uses this information to guide the future of all Universalist worlds."

"Why hasn't this system of forecasting provided answers to the problems we're facing here?" I asked.

A sad look darkened Nordel's bright good looks.

"The Council doesn't consider this planet to be one of their worlds. Evidently they set up this culture and society to be a self-sustaining service organization for them. The Council doesn't give this world the same status they give the twenty two Universalist worlds. I'll have more information on the relationship between our world and the Universalist Council in the near future. I've got our best Game players working on it."

After a few more questions and answers, the meeting wound down. Many of the attendees seemed to be in a state of shock, with minds numbed by what they'd learned. I was familiar with the feeling, even getting accustomed to it. But that didn't mean I liked it. The situation was somewhat parallel to the Rainbow Room. That which appeared to be solid could collapse at any time. I wanted a mental map of factual information about the culture to replace the misinformation that was being peeled away, layer by layer.

A short time later I was talking with Clandine and Arvon, when they were notified by a VIS officer that Dreena had been arrested and was being brought to the overseers' urbode for vericator questioning.

Arvon asked, "Any sign of Errox?"

"No. But we found a green wristlock in Dreena's dwell. It looks like Errox is running free with a rainbow wristlock."

I went with Clandine and Arvon to the vericator room. Nordel, Yondoka, Incate, and Prevance were waiting there. Dreena lay on a cot with the vericator skull cap and sensors attached to her. The scene reminded me of being in the VIS station when the dying Freedom Crusader was being questioned. The difference was that Dreena was not dying, but she knew that unless she cooperated her individuality—her personality and character—would be dissolved by a brainwiping machine.

"Did you put a rainbow wristlock on Errox?" Clandine asked.

"Yes, I did."

"Do you know where he is now?"

"No, I don't."

"When did he leave your dwell?"

"Early. He came back not long after he and Rathe had left. He had a rainbow wristlock that he wanted put on him right away. I put it on and he left."

"Where did he go?"

"I don't know."

"Are you his lover?"

"Yes, I am."

Arvon touched Clandine on the shoulder to indicate that he wanted to ask a question. Clandine yielded.

"Are you a Freedom Crusader?" Arvon asked.

Dreena paused for a long time before answering with "Not exactly. That's Errox's scam."

"What do you mean by a scam?"

"Errox obtained the names of people who had a potential for explosive violence and convinced them to become Freedom

Crusaders. Errox doesn't believe in the nonsense he tells them. It's a scam. One of Errox's projects designed to give him more power."

"Where does Errox get the names?"

"From Simulike data that records who welcomes violence and from Flantel, who gives him the names of people who have confessed violent urges to the clergy. Flantel was supposed to turn the names over to Wanklurm so the violent ones could be re-educated or brainwiped. Errox learned that Wanklurm was turning some of these people into members of his elite guard—those troops that wear the white caps—so he decided to form his own group of true believers with a taste for violence or martyrdom."

Yondoka asked, "Are the elite guards used for assassination?"

"Errox says they are. That's all I know about them."

When Yondoka turned away, Arvon asked, "Did you and Errox make any plans to meet anywhere other than your dwell?"

"No, he just comes by whenever he wants to see me."

"Where is his dwell?"

"I don't know where he stays when he isn't with me."

The believability line on the vericator never dipped. Dreena was telling the truth as she knew it.

Prevance asked, "Did he say anything to you about Cainenol?"

"Only that it would help get the Freedom Crusaders ready."

"Ready for what?"

"To go to war with Wanklurm and the elite guards. Errox wants to kill them all and then put himself, or someone who is loyal to him, into Wanklurm's spot as VIS chief."

"Do you think he can do that?" Prevance asked.

"I don't know," she answered. "He thinks he can. So far, he's done things that others thought were impossible. Just before Transit Day he was a gray. Now he's a rainbow."

I recalled what Boget had said about Errox, that he was a person of limitless ambition. Incate and Prevance took their turns questioning Dreena. They established that Dreena didn't know where the Cainenol was stored in the Simulike Palace. She didn't know anything about where Errox kept it, had never taken Cainenol, and knew nothing about it that wasn't common knowledge in the urbodes.

Clandine asked me if I had any questions to ask of Dreena. I stepped forward and asked, "Dreena, had you ever seen me before Boget brought me to your dwell?"

"No, I hadn't."

"Had you heard of me from Errox?" I asked.

"Yes. He told me about you."

"What did he tell you?"

"That you'd been brainwiped and dumped in the Rainbow Room to die."

"Did he know why I'd been brainwiped?"

"If he did, he didn't tell me."

"Did he say anything at all about me being brainwiped and dumped?"

"He said that he thought Wanklurm had done it. Probably he didn't want your body showing up in the Medical Complex where someone might recognize you or connect you to him."

"What made you summon Errox after Boget brought me to you for a white wristlock? Had Errox told you to be on the lookout for me?"

She shook her head. "Not you specifically. Errox asked me to contact him if Boget or any other rainbow brought around anyone for a new wristlock."

I didn't have any more questions. Arvon had a few more questions about the Freedom Crusaders but didn't get any new information. When he finished his questions, I motioned him aside and asked, "What's being done about the Rainbow Room? The whole Color Wheel is a deadly hoax. People are risking their lives for a run at the rainbow, seeking an immortality that doesn't exist."

"We closed the Color Wheel down, ostensibly for repairs. We intend to demolish it without ever opening it again."

I found that information very reassuring. My experiences in the Rainbow Room and other parts of the Color Wheel were memories that I hoped would fade in time. Once the building was destroyed maybe those experiences wouldn't come into my mind every time I passed the site.

Eventually Dreena was disconnected from the vericator and led away by two VIS officers.

I asked Clandine what was going to happen to Dreena.

"She'll be put in a holding cell for now. Later she'll be examined at the Medical Complex. The medics will decide whether or not she can be rehabilitated by a re-education program."

"And if she can't?"

"Then she'll be brainwiped, given a new appearance along with a new name, and she'll start life all over."

"Oh," I replied, hiding my own feelings on the subject. Clandine's casual attitude about having all of one's memories eliminated bothered me a lot. I wondered how dismissive Clandine would be about brainwiping if it were done to her.

"Rathe, you seem fatigued. Let me get a dwell assigned to you here in the overseers' urbode so you can get some rest."

I acquiesced. I was exhausted from trying to assimilate all the new information I had learned today.

SEVENTEEN

Although I was exhausted, I slept only a short time in the dwell assigned to me in the overseers' urbode. My dreams had been chaotic, consisting of hurried trips on dead end slideways, whispered directions of confusing complexity and unexpected twists to any path I took. I awoke in a sweat. I cleaned myself and took a fresh tunic from the ample supply in the dwell.

As I ate some food cubes, I pondered about what I could do to aid the Alliance. I could recognize Errox on sight but I had no idea where to find him. I didn't want to see him, just locate him so I could tell the Alliance where he was so they could arrest him for the murder of Boget. Errox wouldn't be in the Simulike Palace because VIS personnel were searching it for the Cainenol supply.

He wouldn't be at Dreena's place because he would have no difficulty discovering that she had been arrested and her dwell was under surveillance. Maybe he was out looking for Ozerta, hoping to learn when the next shipment of Cainenol was coming in. I didn't think he knew that the Cainenol had been stopped at the source.

I mentally reviewed all the people I had met who were acquainted with Errox. Only one, other than Dreena, seemed to know much about him. That person was Kahalyton of the Counter

Colors. I remembered him saying to me about Errox, "Someday when I've drunk my fill of jarva, I will tell you about him."

I needed to find Kahalyton, but I had no idea of the location of his dwell or how to get in touch with the Counter Colors who would know. I wished that I could access the Delphic method techniques and get some direction, some oracular information full of sage advice. Sage! Kahalyton had appeared in my Simulike experience as a sage. Maybe there was something I could recall from that episode that would lead me toward Kahalyton.

I stopped pacing, sat down, and took deep, even breaths. I reviewed the entire encounter in my mind. I remembered meeting the sage at a bend in the path. He told me that death didn't lie and gave me a vision to help me understand, a vision in which a rainbow turned upside down. I couldn't identify any rainbow that had been turned upside down although the Alliance was working toward ending the rainbow status of Flantel, Ozerta, and Wanklurm. Boget had been upended in the sense that he had died, verifying the sage's statement that the apparition representing death did not lie.

The bend in the path where I found the sage, what did it represent? All the walkways were straight. There were no bends. Then I remembered walking through the Medical Complex where I'd seen an outdoor pavilion and a path that curved around it. Was I reading more into my Simulike experience than it contained? I didn't know but I was going to find out.

I took two jars of jarva from the supply cabinet in the dwell, put them in my waist pouch, and went to the Medical Complex pavilion in search of Kahalyton. Twilight was deepening as I walked along the curving path. I could hear a voice but I could not understand the words. It wasn't Kahalyton's voice. It was a woman's voice. As I got closer I could see her, a gray-haired woman speaking to a small group who gave her their attention. I realized that she was one of the gray storytellers I had heard of. I sat down in the back of the group.

The storyteller noticed me joining the group but she didn't stop telling the audience her tale. When I heard her next words I realized that she was winding up her story. She said, "So many ages ago on a world called Arth, four people—Dotto, Scarow, Tinmun, and Lineguy—penetrated the illusions of the wizard and found a new reality that enabled them to live happier and more fully, cherishing what they had learned and sharing it with others."

I joined in the applause when she stopped speaking. Some of her audience left. Others clustered around her, expressing their appreciation of the entertainment. When I got a chance to speak to her I said, "I regret that I didn't arrive in time to hear the entire tale."

She looked at my white wristlock and said, "I'm surprised that you showed up."

"Do you know me?"

"No. It's just that my audience has always consisted only of grays. How did you learn about our gathering?"

"I didn't. I came here looking for a way to contact a friend named Kahalyton. Can you help me?"

"Who are you?" she asked.

"My name is Rathe. Kahalyton befriended me when I was a blanc."

"You were a blanc and now you wear a white wristlock?" She studied me curiously out of owl-like eyes.

"Yes. I'm now a member of the Alliance."

"Is your friend Kahalyton also a member of this Alliance?"

"No, he's a member of the Counter Colors. I want to give him some information I've learned from the Alliance and get his help in locating someone the Alliance wants to find."

Most of the members of the audience had drifted away, having recognized that the storyteller and I were engaged in a serious discussion that precluded small talk interruptions. I wanted the storyteller to trust me. I said, "I know from Yondoka and Nordel that the Alliance is promoting folk tales intended to help prepare people for the changes that must take place in this culture. I want to help the Alliance and the Counter Colors communicate with each other."

"Wait right here," she said, before walking over to a man and woman who had been listening to her story. I was unable to overhear what she said to them. They talked briefly.

Then the three of them came over to where I was waiting. The storyteller said to me, "These people will take you to a meeting place. Perhaps you'll find someone there who will help you."

She hadn't introduced me to the couple nor had she told me her name. It was just another indication of the rising level of tension in the society—not telling strangers your name as a way of preserving anonymity, a way of keeping distance between yourself and the people who might have power over you if they knew who and where you are.

The storyteller left.

The woman took a strip of tunic out of her waist pouch and said, "You'll have to be blindfolded if you want to go with us."

I nodded my agreement.

She put the cloth over my eyes. I tried to keep a surge of paranoia from overpowering me. I was giving my trust to strangers, but I felt I had no other option that would lead me anywhere.

"What do you have in your waist pouch?" It was the deep voice of the man who hadn't spoken previously.

"Just some jarva for Kahalyton." I felt his hands search my waist pouch and establish that I had told the truth.

He took me by one arm and she by the other. They led me away from the pavilion, taking many turns and sometimes doubling back part way over the previous route. By the time we reached a slidestrip I had no sense of what direction we were going in or where we were in relation to the mental map I had put so much effort into making. Once on the slideway the couple kept me between them. I saw nothing because of the blindfold. I wondered if any other slidestrip travelers noticed my blindfold. Then I remembered that it was twilight time and unless we approached someone no one would notice.

Even if they did, they would probably assume we were playing some kind of a game or conducting an initiation. It didn't feel like a game to me. Eventually we got off the slideway. They led me to a walkway and then to a dwell in an urbode.

I was still wearing my blindfold when I heard Kahalyton's voice say, "Yes, that's my friend Rathe. You can leave us alone."

I heard several people leave. Then Kahalyton spoke, "Welcome, Rathe. You can take off the blindfold."

The light was dim, but it still hurt my eyes briefly. When they had adjusted, I looked at Kahalyton. He didn't look quite the same, a bit tired perhaps, as if he hadn't slept well for several days.

"Hello, Kahalyton. I'm glad to see you."

He looked down at my wrist. "Rathe, I see you have a white wristlock. I was hoping that you had come to join the Counter Colors but you seem to have taken a different path."

"I think our paths may converge." I took the jarva out of my waist pouch and handed him a bottle. "You once told me that sometime when you had your fill of jarva you would tell me about Errox. I'd like for you to tell me now. I need to find him."

"Errox will be hard to find these days. Wherever he is, you can be positive that he will be protected by his brainwashed Freedom Crusaders. Dealing with them can be dangerous. They are true believers who can't hear or understand any questions that the rhetoric they'd been fed doesn't answer. I think it would be dangerous for anyone other than a Crusader to approach Errox right now."

"I don't want to approach him. I want to locate him to report his whereabouts to the people who are interested in stopping him from distributing Cainenol. I want to know anything you can tell me about Errox."

Kahalyton and I both drank some jarva. Then Kahalyton said, "I'll tell you what I know about Errox, but in exchange you must tell me what you know about Cainenol. You seem to have information that confirms some of my suspicions. Is it a deal? Do we trade information?"

"Yes, we've got a deal," I replied.

"I first met Errox when he was seeking personal power among the permanent grays. Several of the Counter Colors had heard about him and suggested that I meet him to see if he might be an asset to our organization. I met and talked with him on several occasions. I never told him of the Counter Colors because I suspected that he was the kind of person who would not join any organization unless he wanted to take it over and run it. I got reports on his associates and activities. I say associates because he had no friends—only people he could use.

"His activities, which included riplocking, showed that he had a flawed character. The man has no moral center. His style is expediency without ethics, maneuvers without morality, reactions without respect." Kahalyton paused, took a sip of jarva, and continued. "He tried running multiple-player schemes in unsuccessful efforts to outsmart the Game, using a smitty so that each player wore the same wristlock when he or she played the Game. When those projects failed he abandoned his cohorts, leaving them in the hands of the VIS. He takes only those lovers who might be useful to him and when their usefulness ends, he discards them like worn out sandals. Have I told you enough or do you need more details?"

"Do you have any information that might help me locate him?"

"No, Rathe, I don't. Tell me what you know about Cainenol. I know that Errox has used it to indoctrinate and control his Crusaders and others."

"Errox entered into a conspiracy with several influential rainbows to import Cainenol so they could use it to increase their power, create love slaves, and turn people into pawns—"

Kahalyton interrupted by asking, "How did you learn of this conspiracy?"

"I was arrested by the VIS who thought I was Errox because I was wearing his wristlock. When they discovered that I was a blanc, one VIS officer convinced me to become an undercover agent who would try to find Errox."

"Are you working for Wanklurm?"

"No, he's part of the conspiracy. I'm working for the Alliance for Cultural Transformation, a group consisting mostly of rainbows and non-corrupt VIS personnel. They called in two off-world rainbows as investigators."

"Off-worlders! Kahalyton exclaimed. "How do they fit in to all of this?"

I quickly told him what little I knew about the off-worlders, and what they had told me.

"Do you trust them?"

"No, I don't. Although they cut off the Cainenol supply at its off-world source, I think they want to downplay the conspiracy and minimize or ignore the problems of this culture."

"So there will be no more Cainenol?" he asked.

"The last shipment hasn't been distributed. Errox probably has it. He's wearing a rainbow wristlock that he took from the

Simulike Palace overseer Boget who was dealing in unauthorized wristlocks."

"What's being done about Boget?"

"Errox killed him to take over the Cainenol trade. I was unconscious when he broke Boget's neck, but I have no doubts that he was responsible."

"Then you should keep your distance from Errox. He would have no compunctions about killing you as well."

"I know," I said, taking a deep breath. "That's a major motivation for finding him and getting him arrested by members of the Alliance. Do you know that Alliance members are the principal suppliers of the folk tales your storytellers relate?"

"I didn't know where their stories came from. I always thought they were just old tales and fables that were useful for instituting change. How did you learn that the storytellers are Counter Colors?"

"I deduced it from the information I had. The storytellers are using their tales to prepare the grays for change, a cause that is dear to your heart. The Alliance has uncovered some of the truth about this society and intends to transform the culture."

"Will you tell me what those truths are?" Kahalyton asked hesitantly, as if he were afraid of what he might learn.

"Yes. I'm sure you suspect many of them already. First of all, this world is one of twenty-three known worlds—"

Kahalyton interrupted again. "Twenty-three worlds? I had heard old tales about other worlds, but I wasn't sure how much truth was in them. Are the other worlds like this one?"

"There are differences, but I don't know how extensive the differences are. The other twenty two are members of the Universalist Council. This world is not; it was set up as a service organization for the Council. This culture and the Game are artificial constructs designed to serve the Council."

"What is the purpose of the Game?"

"The Game produces forecasting information that the Council uses for administering the other twenty-two worlds. The culture of this world is filled with deceit and beliefs that can't be verified."

"Like the religion?" he asked. "I found little value in spiritual exercises that are supposed to make the next reincarnation better."

"Reincarnation is unproven. The humans that emerge from the House of Rebirth are blancs, brainwiped people, sent here from the twenty-two worlds; they are not reincarnations of people who have died on this world."

"Why are they brainwiped?"

"I don't know, but I mean to find out. I'm beginning to suspect they're subversives or political outcasts of some sort. People who don't conform to the norms of their world."

Kahalyton nodded as if that assessment agreed with his own.

I continued, "Getting people to compete in the Game for rainbow status is a cruel hoax. Rainbows are not reincarnated. They just get periodic rejuvenation treatments."

He looked at me with newfound respect in his eyes. "You've learned in a short time much of what we Counter Colors either knew or suspected. You must have been someone special before you were brainwiped. What does the Alliance you belong to intend to do about it?"

"They are going to arrest the other conspirators and transform the culture as best they can. Their plans aren't final. There are still too many questions to be answered."

"Who are the other conspirators?" he asked.

"So far we've identified Errox, the late Boget, Ozerta of the House of Rebirth, Flantel who oversees the clergy and Wanklurm."

"How are they going to deal with Wanklurm?"

"I'm not sure but the Alliance has ascertained that most of the VIS personnel, other than the elite guard, have not been corrupted and will cooperate in neutralizing Wanklurm. When that happens, I hope there can be a closer relationship between the Alliance and the Counter Colors."

"I hope so, Rathe. In the meantime, I'll get the Counter Colors looking for Errox discretely. If I learn anything, how do I contact you?"

"My dwell is in the overseers' urbode. There's always someone there to take messages if I'm out. How do I find you, if I have more information for you?"

"I'll let all the storytellers know that you can be trusted. At twilight every evening, storytellers can be found outside most public buildings and on the front walkway of almost every urbode section. Any storyteller can arrange another meeting like this."

I talked with Kahalyton a while longer and we both drank a bit more jarva before he left with Counter Color friends.

A tall, lean man with piercing gray eyes told me that he would escort me from the meeting place to a location I would recognize.

He put the blindfold on again before we left. When my guide took the blindfold off and bid me goodbye, I was on a slidestrip that was near the Simulike Palace. I was checking my mental map to determine the best route to the overseers' urbode when two of Wanklurm's elite guards, wearing their distinctive white caps, began moving from the adjacent slidestrip to the slowstrip I was on. They were looking all around, as if seeking suspects or trouble.

As I attempted to look as innocent and trouble free as I could, a group of five or six grays clustered around the white caps and a scuffle ensued.

I got off the first exit slidestrip, but not soon enough to miss seeing two white-capped bodies thrown over the side as someone yelled, "Freedom forever!"

I saw other white caps moving over to the slowstrip I had just left. One of them said in an authoritative voice, "Officers down. Search the area. Arrest anyone you see. Kill anyone who looks like a Crusader."

I scrambled under the slidestrip, knowing my life was in danger. I had to find a safe place. I could hear the white caps but I couldn't tell whether they were pursuing me or someone else. Then I heard an explosive sound, not as loud as a wristlock exploding. I saw a body fall just to my right. I realized that the sound I heard was made by an illegal bolt gun, a device I'd heard about from Kahalyton but had never seen. I tried to get back on the slideway but I was on the far side, next to the fast strip. I jumped on, trying to run as I hit. I tumbled, lost a sandal, and felt my tunic rip as I fell off the strip.

I hadn't traveled far enough to be out of danger. I had to get away from public places and open spaces. Where could I go? The answer suddenly came to me—Boget's dwell. It was in the right neighborhood and my wristlock would open the door.

I kicked off the other sandal hoping I'd look like a barefoot enthusiast rather than someone who'd lost a sandal. I tucked part of my tunic into the waist pouch to conceal the rip. I stayed in the shadows, moved cautiously down the slideway, and kept alert. Only when I was safely inside Boget's dwell was I able to resume normal breathing.

I put my torn tunic in the recycle slot. I cleansed myself and put antiseptic new skin on my knees and elbows. I took a new tunic and a pair of sandals from Boget's closet. I started to put them on and then realized that I was safer from the elite guards here than I would be traveling to the overseers' urbode. The sleep platform looked very inviting.

I helped myself to some of Boget's jarva and lost myself in sleep. I hoped I wouldn't dream of running from the elite guards. My dreams were of Lyonella. She came to me like a succubus that hovered over me in the darkness. I couldn't make out her features but I felt her presence. I was lying on my back.

In a voice so hoarse with passion that I hardly recognized it, she said, "Lie still. I will do everything."

She aroused me quickly, mounted me, and began a series of sensual motions—clenching and releasing, drawing me into her warm wetness, bracing herself by pressing her hands against my wrists as if to hold me to the platform while she rocked back and forth. I could feel my imminent climax building. Everything seemed so real, I could scarcely believe it was a dream.

In a throaty, breathless voice she said, "Now. With me. Both of us together." Everything happened at once. I felt her climax along with my own.

Suddenly, the lights came on.

I was looking into the face of Ozerta.

A voice from the doorway said, "You're under arrest."

I recognized the voice—it was Incate's.

EIGHTEEN

Ozerta recovered before I did. I was shocked that this hadn't been a dream, that my sexual partner was not Lyonella, and that Incate and Prevance had entered Boget's dwell. I lay on the sleep platform stunned while Ozerta calmly got up and slipped a tunic over her well-shaped body. She said to Incate and Prevance, "Who are you and what are you doing here?"

Incate started to speak but Prevance restrained him and said, "My name is Prevance. My partner's name is Incate. We are special investigators sent here by the Universalist Council—"

Ozerta stepped into her sandals, smoothed her blonde hair back from her face, and interrupted with, "I'll get Boget or Wanklurm to straighten this out."

Then looking at me, she asked, "Where's Boget?"

Incate answered, "Boget's dead. Your friend here knows that. The last time we were in this dwell we found him here with the corpse. What are you doing here? Replacing an old lover with a new one?"

Ozerta, looking down her nose at Incate, asked, "Do you know who I am?"

Her haughty tone reminded me of the bickering couple in my Simulike experience; she was the woman of that couple.

Incate answered, "You're Ozerta, overseer of the House of Rebirth. You are being arrested for conspiracy."

Ozerta addressed both investigators. "Do you two think I had something to do with Boget's death? I've been in the Fane of Change. When I was ready to leave, I was given a message from Boget saying he had a surprise for me. I came here and was surprised to find my lover waiting for me. He's been missing for some time. I was afraid that Wanklurm had imprisoned him."

Turning to me, as I was rising from the sleep platform, she asked, "What happened to you, Tannet? What kept you away from me?"

I was confused by her questions. The only memory I had of Ozerta was the pixcube that Clandine had showed me. Prevance spoke before I could gather my thoughts and produce an answer. He said, "You know this man as Tannet?"

"Yes. He's a very important person. He's going to become a rainbow and be the new overseer of the clergy."

"He claims to be a blanc who took the name of Rathe," Incate said. "I think he's found some drug that enabled him to beat the vericator."

Ozerta looked at me and asked, "What's going on here, Tannet? Tell them who you really are."

"The only name I have for myself is Rathe. I entered this life as a nu-blanc, dumped into the Rainbow Room to die. I managed to survive. Boget got me this white wristlock and wanted me to help run the Simulike Palace."

I saw sadness in Ozerta's expression as she asked, "You have no memory of me, of being a master Game player, of our plans for the future?"

"I'm sorry. No."

She turned to Incate, her face red, saying, "Wanklurm and his crazy jealousy! We argued a lot but I never thought he'd try to stop my affair with you by such drastic means. He must have done it. Had you brainwiped and dumped in the Rainbow Room. He knew that if your body had turned up in the Medical Complex, I would have heard about it. Boget must have recognized you and befriended you so you and I could be together again."

That explained two things: why I had been left to die after being brainwiped and why it had been so easy for me to insinuate myself into Boget's life. He had recognized me and thought he was doing a favor for Ozerta. He had me stay in his dwell so Wanklurm wouldn't know I was still alive.

Now I knew who my enemy was—Wanklurm, the most powerful person on the planet. Ozerta said they had argued, a verbal confirmation that she and Wanklurm were the bickering couple in my Simulike experience.

Prevance said, "It's time for all of us to go to the overseers' urbode and investigate this further."

Ozerta asked, "You still think I had something to do with Boget's death? That's unreasonable. He was my friend."

Incate said, with a triumphant note in his voice, "You are being arrested for conspiracy to import and distribute Cainenol."

Ozerta's face fell. Her posture sagged. Prevance halfway supported her as we headed for the door.

Incate said, "I've got a stun gun to make sure that all four of us get where we're going." He glanced at me as he said it. His suspicions and hostility toward me had not been diminished by this episode.

On the slideway Ozerta asked me, "Who killed Boget and why?" I answered, "Errox. He wants to take Boget's place."

Ozerta said scornfully, "That little gray upstart. Wanklurm will kill him."

"That's enough talk until we get you hooked up to a vericator," Incate said.

He was looking at Ozerta as he said it, but I knew that he didn't believe I was telling him the complete truth.

When we got to the overseers' urbode, Ozerta demanded that Wanklurm be notified that she was under arrest. Prevance told her that wasn't going to happen. He didn't tell her that he knew Wanklurm was part of the Cainenol conspiracy. I was careful not to reveal anything to Ozerta. I didn't want to increase the suspicions that Incate, and perhaps Prevance, had about me.

The vericator session with Ozerta was attended by Incate, Prevance, Yondoka, Nordel, Arvon, and me. Everyone had been briefed on the situation including my part in it. I knew that my story would be verified if I submitted to a vericator session, but I wanted to be trusted without being tested.

I hoped that Ozerta's session would confirm at least part of what I'd revealed about seeking contacts in the gray community to locate Errox, as well as going to Boget's dwell to avoid the elite guards who were looking for someone who had killed one of their number.

I asked where Clandine was and was told she was pursuing a possible lead on the location of Flantel. According to cleric sources, Flantel was away on a spiritual retreat. I remembered his rampant sexuality on All Hues Day. Evidently he found sexuality and spirituality compatible.

Prevance started the questioning, "Ozerta, you are accused of conspiring with Boget, Flantel, and Wanklurm to import and distribute Cainenol. Do you admit your guilt?"

"No," she answered, her voice firm.

"Do you deny your guilt?"

"I have no reason to admit or deny anything."

I was surprised by Ozerta's response. I'd been the subject of two vericator sessions and I'd observed two others, one with the dying Crusader and the other one with Dreena, the smitty. I'd told the truth because it seemed like the only course to follow. The dying Crusader was certain that she would be reborn in paradise and she knew that she had no information that would damage the Freedom Crusaders so she had no reason to be reticent. Dreena was truthful because she knew nothing that would be disadvantageous to her lover Errox. She had been working at an illegal trade for some time and may have been prepared for eventual discovery and arrest.

But Ozerta was skilled in dealing with the vericator session. She neither confirmed nor denied, giving nothing away. She was being defiant even though she must be without hope. Prevance asked a few more questions without any significant results. Yondoka tapped him on the shoulder to indicate she would take over the interrogation. Prevance stepped back. Incate glared at Yondoka.

Yondoka said, "Ozerta, I understand your reluctance to answer questions. We know that you, Boget, Flantel, and Wanklurm conspired to bring in Cainenol. Boget is dead. Flantel will soon be under arrest. We are formulating plans to arrest Wanklurm as soon as that can be done with a minimum of violence. We don't need your testimony to convict anyone. What we do want is information that will help us transform this culture into one that is based on truth and responsible freedom. We would like your help. Do you have any questions that you'd like the answer to?"

Ozerta looked at Yondoka and asked, "What's going to happen to me?"

"You won't be allowed to continue living as Ozerta," Yondoka said. "You'll be subjected to memory removal. Your appearance will be altered to conceal your previous identity and you'll start life over."

"So I'm to be brainwiped, reassembled and made to live on this planet again."

"Yes."

"I want the suicide option. I want your guarantee that if I answer all your questions, you will allow me to use the suicide chamber in the Medical Complex."

I hadn't known there was a suicide chamber. There were a lot of things I didn't know.

"The suicide option is yours if you want it. Will you tell me why that is your choice?"

"I don't want another life as a prisoner."

"You won't be a prisoner," he said. "You'll be as free as the rest of us."

Ozerta said, in a louder than normal voice, "You people don't know you are prisoners. All of you. This is a prison planet. We are all imprisoned here because we are the genetic undesirables from the twenty-two Universalist planets."

I looked at the monitor and saw that she believed what she was saying. I felt as if someone had thrown cold water in my face. We had all been judged undesirable on a genetic basis.

Yondoka appeared shocked. Nordel looked pensive.

Arvon kept his face impassive but his posture became rigid.

Prevance and Incate exchanged looks with each other. I wasn't sure what those looks meant but I was certain that they were displeased about what was being revealed.

"Genetically undesirable in what way?" Nordel asked.

Ozerta took a deep breath and said, "All of us sent here have a genetic combination that makes us potentially capable of possession—taking over the mind and body of another human being for a short time and imposing our will. I was given the whole history by Wanklurm when I became a rainbow. The Universalists used to kill us in the early days; until they discovered that the same genetic combination included a potential for forecasting the future. To utilize these predictive abilities, the Universalist Council set up this planet as a self-sustaining prison with a culture that discouraged any change and offered the cruel illusion of upward mobility."

The believability line on the monitor never wavered. What Ozerta was saying fit with what Nordel had revealed previously, that the Game was nothing more than an elaborate forecasting system.

Arvon looked at her in disbelief. "If we have this possession ability, why aren't there any manifestations of it here on this planet?"

Ozerta replied, "The machines that harness the tidal energy emit a frequency that blocks possession here and keeps the possession signals from leaving the planet. The Simulike machines were intended to guide the possession energy into dreamlike sequences in order to keep the population content. Some time ago it was discovered that a design flaw allowed some people to overcome the frequency blockers.

"When Boget learned that he would be getting new Simulike machines, he thought it would be a perfect opportunity to import Cainenol, a drug he thought would be interesting for experimental use. Boget thought he could bring Cainenol in first with the machines and then later with the blancs sent to the House of Rebirth. That's when he, Flantel, Wanklurm, and I decided we would get our revenge on the Universalists.

"Boget loved the intrigue. Flantel wanted Cainenol to create love slaves. Wanklurm wanted to become ruler of the planet and threatened to dismantle the Delphi units unless the Universalist Council met his demands. I merely wanted to live the rest of my life as a queen; my compensation for the hard work I performed to become a rainbow—only to find that the eternal life I'd been promised was a fraudulent deception."

Yondoka responded in a kindly voice, "Ozerta, it must have been terribly disturbing for you to realize that the House of Rebirth was merely a receiving station for the unwanted people from the Universalist worlds."

She nodded with tears welling in her eyes. "I turned the day-to-day operations over to my associates. I could no longer stand to see the blancs arrive in their pods—fully grown but brainwiped and sterilized like the rest of us so we can't reproduce."

A perplexed Yondoka asked, "What do you mean by fully grown, sterilized and can't reproduce?"

Ozerta asked, "You don't know how human beings are created?"

"Reincarnation is what I always believed, until I just heard we were blancs from other worlds. Now I don't know. Tell me."

"Human beings are created through sexual intercourse. When a man's ejaculate enters a woman's vagina, there is a substance in the ejaculate that can combine with eggs that are sometimes present in the woman's body. This combination, when it exists, forms a tiny human within the woman's body. This is called reproduction. After three seasons, the tiny human emerges from the vagina. Over a long period of time the tiny human becomes larger and larger. When the process halts, the human is considered fully grown, like all of us.

"Sterilization is the medical process that ends the capacity of humans to produce the substances that can create a tiny human."

The monitor said she was telling the truth but I found it difficult to comprehend. I had experienced sexual relations with

Lyonella and with Ozerta. It seemed inconceivable to me that such an act could have such far-reaching consequences. I wasn't the only one having trouble digesting this information.

Yondoka and Nordel had reached out to hold hands; both seemed to be in a state of confusion.

Arvon's head was angled toward his left sandal. His facial expression was troubled, as if lost in thought.

Prevance and Incate glanced at each other as both of them endeavored to reveal nothing by their facial expressions. I was certain that this was not new information for them. After the initial shock of Ozerta's information wore off, I said, "Incate and Prevance. You already knew this, didn't you?"

Incate blustered.

Prevance said, "We were not authorized to tell you. We were instructed to avoid revealing anything that might disrupt this culture."

"Are you two sterilized genetic undesirables also?" I asked.

They both nodded.

"How does the Universalist Council prevent possession actions on your part?"

Prevance answered, "We have implants that block the signals."

"Enough," Nordel ordered. "We'll discuss this later and decide if the two of you should be subjected to separate vericator sessions. Does anyone need more information from Ozerta?"

No one did. I think we all had gotten more information than we had been ready to absorb.

Nordel asked Ozerta, "How soon do you want to utilize the suicide chamber?"

"As soon as I can be disconnected from this machine and given a chance to clean up and get a fresh tunic."

Incate said, "I'll accompany her to the Medical Complex."

Yondoka, ignoring Incate, asked, "Who would you like to escort you, Ozerta?"

"Just Tannet, whom you know as Rathe."

I nodded acceptance and said, "I'll wait in the lounge until you're ready."

By the time I'd finished a cup of cokafa, Yondoka entered the lounge with Ozerta. Ozerta and I went to the Medical Complex, followed at a discrete distance by Arvon, who was to make sure that Ozerta didn't try to escape. I wasn't sure that Arvon was needed because Ozerta's manner indicated that the only thing she wanted to escape was this life.

In the Medical Complex, she held both my hands, looked into my eyes, and said, "I'm sorry it didn't work out, but what you and I had together are the best memories I have of this life."

"I only wish I shared your memories," I said sadly, knowing I was about to lose the only person who truly knew who I had once been.

She stepped into the chamber and was gone. Along with my past....

NINETEEN

When I returned from the Medical Complex to the overseers' urbode, there was a visitor waiting for me, a slender, brown-haired woman with brown skin and a gray wristlock who introduced herself as Quenlu and told me she would take me to Kahalyton who wanted to see me. I left with her.

There were very few people traveling on the slideway. I commented on this and Quenlu said, "Kahalyton has advised all the Counter Colors to make no trips unless they are essential because they might be mistaken for Crusaders. Wanklurm's white caps are killing suspected Crusaders on sight. They're using those guns that shoot a lightning bolt. Once you're hit, it's permanent cardiac arrest."

"Are we in danger?"

"Probably not," she answered. "Your white wristlock identifies you as not being a Crusader—they're all grays. If we were both grays the guards would probably stop us as suspects and kill us."

We changed slidestrips. At the slideway interchange there was a pair of VIS patrolling. A group of four elite guards entered the interchange. Both groups avoided making eye contact with each other. The white caps got on behind us. My guide leaned close to me and said, "Time to put on the show. Kiss me and pull up my tunic enough to show my rump. Put your hand on it. Make certain that the white caps see your white wristlock against my brown bottom. They'll think you're a Listener or a Cleric with a sexually interested client."

I'm sure the kiss and fondling convinced the elite guards that we were a couple headed to a private spot for sexual intimacy. I found myself almost convinced after the second kiss aroused me. The guards saw my condition as we moved to a slower strip and they passed by us.

When they were out of sight, my guide gently removed my hand from her body, restored her tunic to achieve coverage, and said, "You played your role well. I'm glad that you support our cause."

I cleared my throat and said, "It takes two for that kind of performance." I wondered if the scene had been necessary to avoid contact with the guards. Then I decided that it didn't matter—it gave me another pleasant memory to store away. We were near the autofactory sector where, according to what I'd learned in the overseers' urbode, solar power ran the machines that utilized local supplies to produce tunics, sandals, food cubes, and the other staples that made this planet self-supporting.

Quenlu asked, "Do you know we're being followed by two rainbows?"

"No. What do they look like?"

"Both big. Both male. One is blond. The other has darker hair."

"I know who they are. I can't figure out how they managed to follow us. They haven't been right on our heels."

"They're probably using a spike mike."

"Spike mike?"

"A small transmitter that they imbed in your tunic. It's keyed to a small tracker. It gives them location and approximate distance. Wanklurm uses them."

"I don't want to lead them to Kahalyton. Let's find the spike mike and disable it."

She turned and smiled. "I think I know something that will work better than that. It will keep them busy while we have our meeting with Kahalyton."

"Lead on, Quenlu. I'll follow."

We took the exit slidestrip and made our way to a large factory building. The portal plate had been breached. We went inside. The building was some kind of recycling center. There were huge bins of various kinds of objects, mostly unidentifiable. Quenlu examined my tunic and found the spike mike imbedded in the back just above the waist. She removed it, showed it to me, and dropped it into a container that was part of a robotic device.

Quenlu explained, "This machine is a locator. It looks for a recycling bin with similar devices so it can deposit this one. Since there is little likelihood of there being other spike mikes here, the search will be long and difficult to track because these buildings are made for robots, not humans. Our followers will be occupied for a while. At least long enough for us to meet with Kahalyton."

Quenlu led us past the recycling complex and eventually onto another slideway. When we got off, we were still in the autofactory zone. Kahalyton was in the fifth building, resting on a cot.

He got up when we came in, greeted us both by name, and asked, "How was your journey? Any difficulties?"

Quenlu answered, "Nothing serious. We were trailed by two rainbows but by now they should be busy tracking their spike mike through the recycling complex."

"Do you know who they are, Rathe?" Kahalyton asked.

"They're the off-world investigators I told you about. They think I'm up to something devious."

Quenlu said, "Aren't we all."

"Quenlu organized the storytellers program along with several other projects." Kahalyton's voice indicated that he thought highly of her. "But come along, Rathe. There's someone else I want you to meet." He motioned for us to follow him toward the rear of the building.

When we arrived at an occupied work station, Kahalyton said, "Rathe, I'd like to introduce you to Shangro."

Shangro was working with tools on a bench. He had a bald head, a weathered face and a friendly smile.

We exchanged greetings and then Kahalyton said, "Shangro, tell Rathe what you know of Errox."

Shangro put down his tools and said, "The man who calls himself Errox did not always have that name. I met him in a distant sector long ago. I saw him several times and was told his name was Vargan—"

"Vargan!" I interrupted, "Vargan. His name was Vargan?"

"Yes. He was an opportunist, ready to take any chance that might give him power over others. He got into trouble with the VIS and disappeared. A season or so later on Transit Day, we happened to take dwells in the same urbode. He introduced himself as Errox. He'd changed his appearance—more muscle, less fat, and he'd let his hair grow. He obviously didn't remember ever seeing me before and I didn't bring it up. He wasn't anyone I cared to associate with."

"Do you know what happened to the original Errox?" I asked.

"I suspect that the original Errox died with some help from Vargan," Shangro answered.

"Do you have any idea where the man who calls himself Errox is now?"

"I haven't seen him but he's probably somewhere with those misguided fools called Freedom Crusaders."

I thanked Shangro, Quenlu and Kahalyton. I told Kahalyton that I had some news. He suggested that the three of us take a walk and let Shangro get back to work. When we were outside, walking down a corridor between two factory buildings, Kahalyton said, "Shangro is one of our design geniuses. He's altering one of the obsolete machines to create devices that neutralize the explosive charge in wristlocks and make them easy to remove. When the Counter Colors are ready, we'll have portal plate breachers and wristlock removers for the color-free society we'll build. Transit Day moving will be an option instead of a requirement."

"I hadn't realized the Counter Colors were so well organized," I said.

"We've had to move up our plans. It's obvious that the growing levels of tension, unrest and ignorance are an indication of cultural crisis. We have to be ready for the changes."

He paused and then said, "You mentioned you had some new information for me. Tell me what you've learned."

"The situation here is more complex and worse than any of us has thought. This world wasn't set up just to be a service organization for the Universalist Council. This is a prison planet. All of us were sent here to be prisoners."

"Are we all criminals then?" Quenlu asked. "Criminals who've been brainwiped and banished?"

I answered, "No, we aren't criminals. We are the genetic undesirables from twenty-two planets. Sent here because our genes indicate that we have the potential for possession, the ability to control another person's mind and body for a short time."

Kahalyton said, "I've never heard of such a thing happening. There's nothing like that in the legends, folk tales, myths and rumors that I've heard."

"I can't imagine taking over anyone else's mind and body," Quenlu said, frowning. "Nor can I imagine somebody taking over mine."

"Why aren't there any manifestations of this kind of possession?" Kahalyton asked.

"The machines that harness tidal power put out a blocking frequency."

"That's good information to have," Kahalyton said. "Some of the Counter Colors have examined those tidal devices. They knew there was a signal output but they hadn't learned its purpose. Do you have any other information for us?"

"Yes. I found out where humans come from," Kahalyton said. "You mean the blancs from other worlds? You told me about that previously."

"No. Here we've been led to believe that human beings are reincarnated. Reincarnation may or may not be factual, but human beings are created by a process that we can't use here because we've been surgically altered."

"Surgically altered how?" Quenlu asked, looking disturbed.

"I got this as verified testimony from Ozerta, the former overseer of the House of Rebirth, just before she entered the suicide chamber in the Medical Complex. The way human beings are made is through sexual intercourse. Chemical substances in the man's ejaculate and eggs in the woman's body sometimes combine to form a tiny human. This tiny human spends three seasons developing in the woman's body and then emerges from the woman's vagina."

"That's the strangest thing I ever heard," Quenlu said. "Why haven't they sent us any of these tiny humans?"

"Over a period of time the tiny humans gradually become our size. When that happens, the possession ability can manifest itself. That's when the Universalists do the surgery, brainwipe the persons, and send them here as blancs, hoping they'll develop the ability to play the Game for the greater glory of the Universalist planets."

Kahalyton shook his head in dismay. "Things are worse than any of us have imagined. The entire culture is bogus, designed by the Universalists so they can benefit from our imprisonment. We've got to change things as soon as we can."

"I'd like to take you two to the overseers' urbode and introduce you to Nordel and Yondoka. They are prominent members of the Alliance for Cultural Transformation. I'm sure they would be willing to work with the Counter Colors."

Quenlu said, "Kahalyton, I know Yondoka. She helped me start the storytellers' project. I think the Alliance needs the Counter Colors and I think we need them."

"You're probably right. I'd like to meet them. Are the white caps still roaming the slidestrips, Rathe? The trip might be dangerous for all of us."

Quenlu said, with a grin, "Why don't we go to the recycling complex and pick up a couple of investigators who are looking for a spike mike. They can be our armed escort."

"That's a wonderful idea," I said, and the three of us went looking for rainbows. We found Incate and Prevance inside a recycling building. They were still tracking the spike mike and were surprised to see me. Incate pulled out his stun gun. Looking at Kahalyton, he said, "Don't move, Errox. You're under arrest."

Prevance had not brought out his weapon. He said to me, "Introduce me to your friends."

I told him, "This man, whom Incate called Errox, is Kahalyton. His associate is Quenlu, a friend of Yondoka. Kahalyton and Quenlu, meet Prevance and Incate. Incate is the one who is trying to decide whether or not to put his stun gun back in his waist pouch. The two of them are partners, the off-world investigators I told you about."

Incate, with barely controlled fury, said, "You're not authorized to tell anyone our true identities."

I replied, "You place a value on ignorance that makes me suspect it is part of your operational method."

Prevance broke in: "Let's not quarrel over unimportant issues. What's really going on?"

"What's going on is that you two followed me when you were supposed to be tracking down Errox. Kahalyton, Quenlu, and I are going to the overseers' urbode to exchange some information with the Alliance. Since there is nothing here for you two, this is your opportunity to be our armed escorts to ensure we have a safe trip."

Prevance looked at Quenlu and asked, "You're a friend of Yondoka, like Rathe said?"

Quenlu replied, "It must be difficult to get results as an investigator when you don't trust information from a reliable source."

Prevance made his face blank and said, "We'll be your escorts."

Incate, looking sullen, put away his stun gun.

The five of us made our way toward the overseers' urbode. The only incident that affected our journey was when we had to change slidestrips and had to wait for the Medical Complex body haulers to take away the bodies of three white caps and five grays who were probably Freedom Crusaders. Once they had them all on portable gurneys, our path was clear. None of us made any small talk for the rest of our trip.

TWENTY

Incate and Prevance left us as soon as we arrived at the overseers' urbode. I suspected that they wanted to avoid seeing Nordel and Yondoka, who might ask them how they happened to be escorting Kahalyton, Quenlu, and me when they were supposed to be looking for clues to Errox's location. Yondoka was glad to see Quenlu again and Kahalyton was introduced to everyone.

We sat down for a discussion of what changes could be made in the culture and how the Counter Colors and the Alliance could work together to achieve mutual goals. I began to have hopes that this world could become a better place for humans.

The discussion stopped when Clandine and Arvon arrived.

Clandine said, "We've discovered that Flantel is at the Clergy Training Center. We're taking along a few extra VIS officers, mostly for protection from Crusaders and elite guards. We want to avoid getting caught in any crossfire between those two groups."

All of us expressed our satisfaction at knowing another corrupt rainbow was about to be taken out of the conspiracy.

Clandine asked, "Rathe, would you like to come along with us? According to what Ozerta indicated, you were being groomed to take his place. He might know some details of your life as Tannet."

I was feeling restless. The discussion had been interesting so far but I felt a need to be moving, to be doing something. I wasn't particularly interested in the life I'd lived as Tannet. That life was over and done with. But I was interested in being part of the team that would bring Flantel to justice.

"Yes, I'd like to go with you."

There were few travelers on the slideways. We saw a few VIS patrols but no white caps. Our trip to the Clergy Training Center was quiet, yet something about it disturbed me. I supposed that it was the absence of fellow travelers. Most people were staying inside their urbodes, waiting for something to happen that told them it was safe to come out and resume their usual lives. I didn't know what that something would be but I had a visceral feeling that I would be part of it.

I thought about the coming interrogation of Flantel, remembering the trial of the religious leader in my Simulike experience and recognizing it had been something of a preview of the planned vericator session. I was somewhat lost in thought as we arrived at our destination. My white wristlock opened the portal of the modified urbode that was the Clergy Training Center.

The seven of us went inside—Clandine, Arvon, four armed VIS escorts, and me—where we were greeted by a receptionist whose muscular development gave him a formidable appearance.

"Welcome to the Clergy Training Center. What is the nature of your visit?"

Clandine answered, "We have come to arrest Flantel. Would you summon him for us?"

The receptionist turned to a small, wiry man who looked like a runner and said, "Inform the appropriate trainer that Flantel is wanted in reception."

We waited. The runner returned. He was followed by a tall brunette who wore her hair in bangs. She was nude except for her fancy sandals with the thick heels and ankle straps. On her right wrist was a gray wristlock. Her left hand held the end of a long leash. The other end of the leash was attached to a collar around the neck of Flantel who was several steps behind her, wearing sandals and his rainbow wristlock but no tunic.

She looked us over and said, "I am the trainer. I understand that you want to take my trainee into custody. Is that correct?"

Clandine answered, "Yes." Then looking directly at Flantel, she said, "Flantel, we are arresting you for conspiring to import and distribute Cainenol. You are to come with us and submit to vericator interrogation."

The trainer said to Clandine, "He's very skilled in submission." Turning to Flantel she said, "Are you ready to leave with these people and take responsibility for your deeds?"

"Yes, Mistress Trainer, I am."

"Then give me the kiss of submission and I will release you to their custody." In smooth, polished movements the trainer lowered the long leash, raised her left leg, and stepped over the leash as Flantel sunk to his knees. In a fluid motion the trainer bent forward from the waist and pulled on the leash until Flantel's face was against her buttocks. A minute later she straightened up and handed the end of the leash to Clandine as she said, "The trainee is now in your custody."

Then she turned and walked out of the reception area. Clandine removed the collar and leash from around the neck of the still kneeling Flantel. She replaced it with a custodial collar she took from her waist pouch. She handed the collar and leash she had removed to the receptionist.

He smiled at her, saying, "You may keep these if you think you might have a use for them."

Clandine looked at him as if memorizing the details of his face and said, "Perhaps at another time. Can you get me a tunic for my prisoner?"

The receptionist handed her a tunic from a rack on his right. He looked at Clandine and said, "Here's a tunic. If you have any other needs, I am at your service."

She thanked him and motioned for Flantel to rise and put on the tunic. Then the eight of us left the Clergy Training Center. I was surprised by the scene I had just witnessed. I had heard that Flantel was involved in the conspiracy because he wanted to create love slaves with Cainenol. Yet in the encounter in the reception area he had been playing the part of the slave. I couldn't understand it. Every bit of information I got seemed to confuse me as much as it informed me. I sometimes had the feeling that I had been reborn yesterday.

Then I realized that this scene related to my Simulike experience—Flantel kissing the buttocks of a gray was symbolic of the rainbow turned upside down.

On the slideway, Flantel asked Clandine, "How may I serve you?"

"Just come along quietly. We'll talk when we reach our destination."

We made the trip over the nearly deserted slideway mostly in silence. At the overseers' urbode the news of Flantel's arrest spread rapidly. The vericator session drew a number of people—Nordel, Yondoka, Kahalyton, Quenlu, Incate, Prevance, Arvon, Clandine, and me. Clandine, whom Flantel seemed to have accepted as his new trainer, said that she would be the interrogator, that if anyone else had questions they would have to wait until she was finished.

Nordel looked at Incate and Prevance as if daring them to raise any objection. The two off-worlders looked displeased but said nothing.

Clandine said to Flantel, "Tell me why you joined the conspiracy."

"Are you commanding me to confess? For almost as long as I can remember I've been telling my Clerics to get their clients to confess so they would feel better. I guess my time has come."

"Who approached you about Cainenol?"

"Boget. He said I could use it to make love slaves. The idea appealed to me."

"What did Boget want from you in return?" she asked.

"At first just the names of any of my Clerics' clients who seemed to be violence prone. I agreed since I deplore violence. In addition the religion usually attracts seekers of a spiritual nature instead of the angry grays who are not content with the cultural conditions. It seemed little enough to do in return for love slaves."

"Did you use Cainenol to make love slaves?"

"Oh, yes. It was very satisfying and stimulating at first. But later I became aware of the problems that come along with Cainenol."

"What problems?"

"I had a problem with my first love slave. After several doses of Cainenol she developed a psychic connection with me that enabled her to sense my presence whenever I was within hailing distance. She could locate me in a blackout orgy. She took to following me everywhere, eager to provide whatever services I needed. It handicapped my style."

"What happened to her?"

"She's at the Clergy Training Center. You talked with her. She was in the role of Mistress Trainer. Once she stopped taking Cainenol she remained eager to please me without being obsessive about it."

Clandine shook in puzzlement. "Are you telling me that once she became drug free she switched from submissive to dominant?"

"Not necessarily. The relationship between trainer and trainee is more complex than it appears to be. The trainer learns from the trainee what actions the trainee gets satisfaction from performing. Then the trainer creates mutual pleasure by commanding the trainee to perform those actions."

Clandine took a minute to absorb the concept that Flantel had just presented. Then she continued with, "You said that Boget at first just wanted the names of violent prone grays. What were you asked for after that?"

"Boget and Ozerta wanted my help in getting other rainbows to join the conspiracy. They said we had to have more people involved or Wanklurm would soon control everything."

"Were you able to add more rainbows to the conspiracy?" she asked.

"No. I'm a great planner of orgies and a fair administrator, but a poor conspirator. I couldn't get the Game overseer to listen to my pitch. People who get deeply involved in the Game tend to lose their interest in the more sensual aspects of life. I talked a bit with Jonter, who was Listener Overseer at the time, but before I could make my pitch he told me about the bad Cainenol experience that Lyonella, one of his best Listeners, had."

Flantel got my full attention when he said the name of Lyonella. I made eye contact with Clandine and made motions with my hands indicating I wanted more details. Clandine, who had suspected Lyonella of being involved in the conspiracy, was as eager for more information as I was.

She said, "Tell me about Lyonella's experience."

"Part of the original shipment of Cainenol fell into the hands of a petty criminal named Vargan, a gray I never met. According to Jonter, Vargan wanted to turn Lyonella into his love slave. He wanted her to tell him the secrets of her clients so he would have power over them. He gave her too many doses of Cainenol and she had bad reactions, including a love/hate psychic connection to Vargan. She became unable to function as a Listener and Vargan dropped her."

That was useful information to me. It established that Lyonella was not part of the conspiracy but a victim of it. It also explained why Lyonella, in our first encounter, mistook me for Vargan. Errox, whom she had known as Vargan, was nearby in Hushel the smitty's dwell arranging to get his wristlock put on me. Lyonella's psychic connection told her he was near. Her confusion, probably caused by Cainenol in her system, led her to believe I was

Vargan. The love and hate she had felt for him was directed toward me while he was in the area.

When my attention returned to Flantel, he said, "Jonter knew the Cainenol effects would wear off in time, even if drug use continues, but he was appalled at what had happened to her and what might happen to others. I reported my failure with Jonter to Boget and Ozerta. One of them must have told Wanklurm because shortly thereafter Jonter was killed. I knew then that I wanted nothing more to do with the conspiracy."

"Did you tell Boget or Ozerta that?"

"No. I was afraid they'll tell Wanklurm and I'd be killed."

Clandine looked at me and then asked, "What do you know of a man named Tannet?"

"He was Ozerta's lover. She never introduced us. I think she was grooming him to be Jonter's replacement, but it could have been me she wanted to replace. He was scheduled to become a rainbow. I think Ozerta told him more about what was really going on than any non-rainbow knew. When I heard that he was missing. I suspect that Wanklurm, who was possessive of Ozerta, had him killed."

If I needed any further confirmation that Wanklurm was my enemy, this was it. The late Ozerta, who had been my lover when I was Tannet, had inadvertently put me in a position that ended my life as Tannet.

Clandine gave me a questioning look. I interpreted it as asking me if I had enough information about Tannet. I nodded to her that I was satisfied.

She continued by asking, "Who else was involved in the conspiracy?"

Flantel said, "Boget, Ozerta, and Wanklurm were the only ones I was aware of. They may have had some minor minions, but if there were other rainbows, I never heard about them."

He paused and then asked, "What's going to happen to us?"

Clandine answered, "Boget was killed by an associate. Ozerta chose suicide rather than being brainwiped and reconfigured. Wanklurm hasn't been captured yet but he will be. When he is he'll be given the choice of brainwiping with reconfiguration or suicide. You get the same options."

Flantel said, "I want to live even if I lose my memory and have my looks changed."

I was not surprised that Flantel took the option he did. He obviously wanted another existence. I suspected that he had hopes for a hedonistic life after the conspiracy was ended. I felt sympathy for this man who had gotten in over his head and was now going to have his head emptied of memories. I had endured that and survived it, but I was angry with Wanklurm, the would-be dictator of the planet, the man who tried to kill me.

I knew that brainwiping and reconfiguration would destroy his present life but somehow that didn't seem enough.

The next questions were about the religion, True Faith Forever. Flantel acknowledged that it was a sham. He said, "True Faith Forever was intended to keep the grays from asking unanswerable questions. Blancs sent here had been brainwiped to remove their memories of ever having a previous existence. They came to life knowing the language, able to walk and talk, capable of dealing with this culture after an imprinting session. Everyone entering this world was told this happened through reincarnation. That wasn't true but it was believable. People developed faith in the religion because they were in a highly gullible state and had no conflicting information. I didn't create the system—I just fit into it as best I could."

The session reminded me of my Simulike experience in which I'd seen the trial of the pink-faced religious leader who had tried to defend a religion created to control rather than benefit its followers.

Clandine finished her interrogation and asked if anyone else had questions for Flantel. I didn't so I excused myself from the session. I had a plan of my own. If I could locate Errox, I might be able to have him and his Crusaders arrested by the VIS. Once Errox was out of the action, we could use all our resources to deprive Wanklurm of his power. The first step of my plan was to reestablish contact with Lyonella. I wanted to use her psychic connection with Errox to locate him.

TWENTY-ONE

After Flantel's interrogation was over, I had a private conversation with Clandine. She showed me a pixcube of Wanklurm because I was one of the few people involved with the Alliance who didn't know what he looked like. He was a stern-faced, black-haired man with small eyes and a prominent jaw. As I had suspected, he had been represented in my Simulike experience as the male of the bickering couple.

That couple represented Ozerta, who had been my former lover, and Wanklurm, who had become my enemy. Seeing the pixcube made him more real to me. At last I had seen a face that I could identify if I saw my nemesis.

I still found it a very strange feeling to know that someone wanted to kill me, kill me for knowledge that I had lost and for actions that I would never remember.

I asked Clandine if she had any lingering suspicions about Lyonella being part of the conspiracy.

"I no longer suspect her. I had previous reports that she was observed under the influence of Cainenol and I thought she might be part of the distribution setup. I sought but never found any confirmation that she gave Cainenol to anyone. From what Flantel said I'm sure that she was an innocent victim of that man named Vargan."

"Good," I said. "Kahalyton introduced me to a reliable member of the Counter Colors who told me that Vargan dropped his identity as Vargan and assumed the identity of Errox by wearing his wristlock. Nobody knows for certain what happened to the original Errox but we safely can assume he's dead. Whether by natural causes or murder we don't know and probably can't find out until we put Errox under the vericator. But the important thing is that Lyonella has a psychic connection with the man she knew as Vargan and we know as Errox. I want to see Lyonella and enlist her aid in finding Errox. I'll need a stun gun to protect myself on the slideway that will take me to Lyonella's dwell. Will you help me?"

Clandine asked me if I thought Lyonella would help. My enthusiastic, positive response seemed to tell Clandine something that was not inherent in my words. She arranged for me to be issued a stun gun.

I put it in my pouch and prepared to see Lyonella. I was excited by the idea of seeing her again, an intense excitement that I recognized as being unrelated to locating Errox.

I ate a few food cubes and waited until Incate and Prevance were busy eating before I left. I didn't want those two following me again. The slideways remained almost deserted. I saw one VIS patrol but I didn't see any of the elite guards until I reached the urbode where Lyonella lived. The sentry I'd seen there before was not in sight. Instead there were two white-capped elite guards standing near the portal. They looked at me, saw my white wristlock, and evidently decided that I was of little interest to them. They probably thought I was a Cleric or a Listener.

I took the elevator to Lyonella's floor. In the corridor there was another white cap standing beside the dwell that was adjacent to Lyonella's. When he saw that my interest was in her dwell and not the one he appeared to be guarding, he relaxed but kept his eyes on me.

Lyonella answered her door. She looked at me as if trying to place my face and asked, "Are you seeking a Listener?"

The white cap was making sure he heard every word. I said to Lyonella, "Yes, I need you to listen to me again."

She admitted me. When I was inside she asked, "How long has it been since I last listened to you?"

I recognized this as her professional manner rather than any kind of recognition or remembrance of me. I said, "It was just after last Transit Day in the autofactory section where the drummers played. I was the man who followed you. I was the masked man who made love with you. My name is Rathe."

"I remember the man who had little memory. It was an encounter I couldn't forget. You told me of being brainwiped. Did you follow my advice?"

"Yes. I got a new wristlock as soon as possible and I have not played the Game. You were quite right in saying that the Game is not what it seems."

"You've learned that for yourself?" she asked.

"Yes. That, and many other things which I'll tell you about."

"Tell me. I'll listen."

"The first thing I must tell you is that our previous encounter was not the first time we met. Just before Transit Day, I was in the urbode where you lived previously. I had been brought there by a man called Errox who was arranging for the smitty Hushel to install a wristlock for me. While Errox was talking to Hushel, I waited in the corridor. You opened your door and mistook me for a man named Vargan. Your manner was very confusing to me."

"I have vague memories of that. I was having a Cainenol flashback. I don't have them anymore. I'm not sure why I mistook you for Vargan. You don't look like him."

"Vargan himself was in the building. You sensed it. You do know whenever he is near you, don't you?"

"Why do you want to know?" she asked, backing away.

"I'm working with a group called the Alliance for Cultural Transformation. We want to locate him so he can be arrested. The man you know as Vargan assumed the identity of a man named Errox. He has killed at least one man in an attempt to take over the Cainenol trade. I'm sure he's killed others. He is also responsible for much of the conflict going on now and is the guiding force behind the Crusaders. We want to find him and stop him."

"I'd like to help. I've managed to recover from the effects of the Cainenol that Vargan dosed me with. He needs to be stopped. What can I do?"

"I suspect that he may be in the Simulike Palace. He knows the place well and has unlimited access. I'd like for you to accompany me there and see if you can sense his presence. We won't go inside. That could be dangerous. I have a stun gun to protect us from elite guards and Crusaders."

Lyonella opened a drawer next to her sleep platform and removed a stun gun. My surprise must have shown on my face. She said, as she put it in her waist pouch, "A good Listener learns how to get whatever she needs. I'm an equal partner in any campaign to thwart the man who tried to change my life with a dangerous drug for his petty purposes. Let's go."

We stepped out into the corridor and summoned the elevator. While we were waiting for it, two elite guards emerged from Hushel's dwell. Hushel looked as if he'd been beaten. We heard one guard say to the other, "He'll tell us where Errox is once we get him into the back room at headquarters."

Just then the elevator arrived. The door opened and a white cap with a reddened face hurried out. He didn't glance in our direction because he was intent on getting the attention of the other two guards. He yelled, "Come on. Errox and his Cainenol-crazed Crusaders are attacking our headquarters."

One guard answered, "Do we bring the prisoner?"

"We don't need him anymore," was the reply from the red-faced white cap.

The guard who had asked the question pointed his bolt gun at Hushel and fired. Hushel dropped to the floor, the life gone from his body. The red-faced man, as if noticing us for the first time, pointed and said, "Kill them. We don't need witnesses."

Lyonella and I leaped into the elevator. The door closed before the guards fired. We got off on the bottom floor. There was no one in sight. We made a fast exit and ran to the nearest exit slidestrip and jumped on. When it joined the slideway, we began moving toward the fastest slidestrip, headed in the opposite direction from Wanklurm's headquarters. We were soon out of sight of the urbode where Hushel had died.

I turned to Lyonella, saying, "I want to go to the overseers' urbode and tell the Alliance that Errox and the Crusaders are attacking the home base of the elite guards."

She said, "Do you want me to go with you? You don't need me to locate Vargan—I guess I should call him Errox now—since you know where he is."

"It could be dangerous to go back to your dwell. The white caps who saw us might return to try to find us and kill us since we're witnesses to murder. I think you should stay for a while in the overseers' urbode where I've got a dwell, stay at least until the danger is past."

Lyonella gave me a bold look and asked, "Are you saying that you want me with you?"

"Yes." I wanted to say more but my tongue seemed thick in my mouth. I remembered the night of drumming and sexual satisfaction. My knees seemed a little weak and I felt feverish. Lyonella was watching me intently.

"Are you remembering the night of the freedom of the masks?"

"It's the best memory of my life." With an enigmatic smile, Lyonella said, "Our lives aren't over yet." She touched me on the arm as she spoke and looked into my eyes. I smiled, not trusting myself to speak, enormously pleased that she had said our lives, as if we shared more than a one-night stand, perhaps a lot more, maybe a mutual destiny.

Her spontaneous touching of me had sent quivers of sensations throughout my body. I don't know how I knew it but I was certain that the touch was an indication of emotions shared, perhaps even an emotional bond. When we arrived at the overseers' urbodes, I immediately went to the room that was serving as the communications center. I reported to Nordel that I'd overheard an elite guard say that Errox and the Crusaders were attacking Wanklurm's headquarters.

Incate said, "Let's send out a runner to get confirmation."

"We've previously received a report of bolt blasts and explosions in that area," Nordel said. "I've already sent armed VIS to investigate. Now we know the conflict has begun. Errox has used the last of the Cainenol to inflame his Crusaders. The battle has begun."

Incate cried, "It's a war! Let them fight it out. Then we can arrest the survivors."

Prevance looked at Incate as if he wanted to say something but his mouth remained closed.

I said, "I saw a white cap kill the smitty Hushel with a bolt gun because they didn't need him any more to try to locate Errox. It was murder."

Kahalyton said, "That's what war is, a series of murders."

Incate looked at me with daggers in his eyes, asking, "Who is the woman with you who's hearing all of our plans?"

I introduced Lyonella to the group. I explained that she was a Listener whom Errox tried unsuccessfully to corrupt with Cainenol when he was known as Vargan.

Yondoka asked Lyonella, "Do you have any information that will help us capture Errox?"

Lyonella answered, "The overdose of Cainenol gave me a psychic connection with him. If he survives the attack on

Wanklurm, I should be able to help locate him. I have my own reasons to be eager to help take him out of the action."

There was a lot more conversation about the armed conflict between the Crusaders and the elite guards. Kahalyton mentioned that his Counter Color scouts had reported that all of the known Crusaders had left their urbodes and none had returned. He also reported that various knowledgeable Counter Colors were prepared to help in the coming transmogrification of the culture.

Quenlu added that all the storytellers had been told to cease outdoor operations until further notice but that their roles would be expanded once hostilities ended.

Arvon reported that the Color Wheel remained sealed but the Simulike Palace was open since the search for Cainenol there hadn't turned up anything. Obviously Errox had found the last of the Cainenol.

Further discussion was interrupted by the arrival of a VIS officer. She said, "I have a report on the conflict between the elite guards and the Freedom Crusaders."

That got everyone's attention. I stepped up closer, right behind Incate and Prevance, to hear better. Neither of the two off-worlders noticed me. I heard Incate whisper to Prevance, "Record this for the Council." I saw Prevance reach into his waist pouch and heard a tiny click.

The VIS officer reported, "There's intense fighting at Wanklurm's headquarters. The elite guards and the Freedom Crusaders are killing each other with bolt guns. The Crusaders outnumber the guards but the guards have more bolt guns. Some of the Crusaders have blown up portions of the headquarters building by exploding their wristlocks and losing their lives in the act. It's mass slaughter. Bolt gun victims' bodies have jammed part of the slideway.

"The area around the building is choked with corpses, many of them bloodied and maimed. Much of the outside of the building and some portions of the inside that were exposed by the explosion are covered with blood and gore. The sound of the bolt guns is like repeating thunder. A stench fills the air, strong enough that people in nearby urbodes are fleeing the area with their tunics covering their noses.

"Wanklurm is inside the building. Errox is commanding his troops from a protected rear position. He is evidently using Cainenol to turn some of his Crusaders into berserkers. It looks like the battle will continue for some time. The outcome is anybody's guess."

The VIS officer's report was concise and evidently quite complete. The answers she gave to questions didn't produce any significant new information. I hadn't thought about the carnage, how hearing about it would distress me. No one knew when the violence would end or who would win. I wanted both of them to lose: Wanklurm, who had arranged for me to be brainwiped and left to die in the Rainbow Room, and Errox, who had almost ruined Lyonella's life and set me up to be a suspect for Boget's death.

I noticed Nordel was getting ready to leave the room. I followed him, caught up with him in the corridor and said, "I'd like to talk to you about suspicious activities on the part of Incate and Prevance."

"Tell me," he said, with both eyes meeting mine.

"When they were supposed to be looking for Errox, they followed me to my meeting with Kahalyton. They traced me with a device called a spike mike imbedded in my tunic. I'd never heard of such equipment, but Quenlu told me that such devices have been used by Wanklurm. I found that very suspicious."

"You said suspicious activities. What else, Rathe?"

"Just now in the communications room, when the VIS officer started her report, Incate whispered to Prevance instructions to record the report for the Council. Prevance evidently had some sort of recording device in his waist pouch. I heard it click on. That made me suspect that they are in frequent communication with the Council. If that's true, they haven't told us and it makes me wonder what else they haven't revealed."

Just then Incate and Prevance came out of the communications room. They both gave rather furtive looks when they saw us together. I spoke to Nordel, as if continuing a conversation about my Simulike experiences, saying: "The Simulike experience I had with the machine in Boget's dwell seemed to be a preview of some of the things I've experienced since. If we could translate Simulike experiences into information for the Game players, we might be able to chart a better course of the future for all of us, providing we had a large enough sample—say, for instance, everyone in the overseers' urbode."

Incate and Prevance nodded to us as they passed.

Nordel said to me, "That's interesting, Rathe. It's something we'll have to try when things settle down."

Incate and Prevance were now out of hearing range. Nordel said to me, "Thanks for telling me your suspicions. I have some also. I'm going to have those two followed."

TWENTY-TWO

After my conversation with Nordel, Lyonella and I had some food cubes. While we ate, I told her about the many things I'd learned since our last meeting.

Lyonella said, "I've heard many strange things from my clients, some of which fit well with what you've told me, but some of the truths that underlie this society are stranger than anything my clients discovered or imagined."

I told her of my suspicions regarding Incate and Prevance.

"I think you're right to suspect them of having some hidden agenda. Prevance seems to be the more reasonable of the two, but he acts like a man experiencing internal conflicts. Incate is filled with hostility and suspicions, eager to believe the worst that he can imagine. He lacks compassion and empathy. I suspect that he has never cared for anyone but himself."

When our food was finished, Lyonella and I went to my dwell. As soon as the door closed we were in each other's arms. Our tunics dropped to the floor. We didn't let go as we moved toward the sleep platform. I reached out and set the light level at twilight. I said to her, "I want enough light to see your face."

She stopped my words with her mouth. Our lovemaking made the previous sexual encounter seem like a prelude. I knew that outside this dwell, beyond the boundaries of this urbode, there was a war going on. But here in the embrace of my lover all the problems of the world seemed remote in time and space. Lyonella and I were experiencing a temporary, separate peace. I felt that the center of the universe was right where we were. Sexual satisfaction brought relief from the tension created by the events of the day.

Lyonella sighed and rested her head on my chest. My left arm was around her. The contentment I felt was so new and so complete that I had no words to express it. We slept.

We were awakened some time later by someone at the portal.

Lyonella got up and looked through the view plate and said, "It's Nordel at our door."

My heart fluttered with unexpected joy when she said, "our door." We slipped into tunics and admitted Nordel.

"Rathe, you were right about Incate and Prevance," Nordel said. "After leaving here, they went to the House of Rebirth. In a concealed room in the transporter section, they established audio contact with the Universalist Council and played the recording made of the report on the battle going on. As soon as they finished, I had them arrested by VIS officers and charged with the variation offense of creating unauthorized historical archives. They will be subjected to separate vericator sessions shortly. I knew you'd want to attend."

Lyonella and I joined the others for the vericator session. Arvon, who was running the session, said, "I'm going to interrogate Prevance first since I believe he will be the more cooperative subject."

After Prevance was connected to the vericator, Arvon began the session by saying, "We observed you and Incate in the act of transmitting a forbidden duplication of a VIS officer's field report. How seriously we take that offense depends on several factors; the most important one in your case is honesty about events and circumstances. You do understand that your status as a Universalist Council investigator does not give you the freedom to commit illegal acts?"

Prevance answered, "I understand."

"Who is the senior partner, you or Incate?"

"Incate," Prevance admitted.

"Did you receive your instructions jointly?"

"No. Incate was briefed on the situation and I received my instructions from him."

"What did he tell you?" Arvon asked.

"That we had to stop the Cainenol traffic with the first step being eliminate the source."

"How did you accomplish that?"

"We inspected everything coming in to the Outpost and discovered which planet it was coming from. We alerted the Council to the source and they sent in their troubleshooters who raided the manufacturers and distributors."

"What were your next instructions?" Arvon asked.

"To come here, find the Cainenol conspirators and neutralize them."

"Neutralize them how?"

"I wasn't told. I assumed they would be brainwiped and reconfigured. They would have to remain here because they have the possession genes."

"Did it occur to you that the conspirators might be killed?" Arvon asked.

"No. I was surprised when we found Boget dead."

"I didn't mean by other conspirators. I meant by you and Incate."

Prevance looked shocked, "I'm not an assassin."

The monitor showed that he was telling the truth.

Arvon asked, "What else did you bring in from the outpost in addition to tracking and recording devices?"

"Nothing that I'm aware of."

"You know nothing about a small respirator arrestor we found in your secret communications room?"

"No!" he cried, looking surprised. The monitor showed he was not lying.

"How long have you known Incate?"

"Not very long. I met him recently, for the first time, when I was assigned to be his partner in the Cainenol investigation."

"What were you told about him?"

"Just that he, like me, had the possession genes and had the new blocking apparatus implanted at the base of his skull so that normals would have nothing to fear. The blocking devices are still new and very expensive. I was told that he had extensive field experience and was known for getting the desired results."

"What were the desired results in this case?" Arvon asked.

"Halt the Cainenol traffic, identify the conspirators, neutralize them, disrupt the status quo as little as possible and keep the Delphic Game players at their tasks."

"Do you think that Incate is an assassin?"

"I don't know. He seems to have very little respect for others, almost as if he feels superior to everyone here. His evident indifference to others may mean that he'd have no reservations about killing someone who stood between him and his objectives."

Arvon asked a few more questions that elicited no new information. He then turned the questioning over to me.

I looked Prevance straight in the eyes. "When was the spike mike stuck in my tunic?"

"I don't know. The first I heard about it was when Incate showed me the tracking device while we were following you to your meeting with Kahalyton and Quenlu."

"Prevance, I've heard that Wanklurm uses spike mikes. Do you think that Incate might be in collusion with Wanklurm?"

"I'd be surprised if he is. I've been with him most of the time we've been here. I don't know when he could have seen Wanklurm."

"Do you know why Incate was so suspicious of me?"

"Incate wanted a rapid solution to the situation. He thought that Boget might be the only rainbow involved. When we found you with Boget's body, he thought he could wrap up the case quickly if Boget was the main conspirator and you were a disgruntled minion who killed him."

I had no more questions. Some of the others asked about Prevance's special status, having a non-possession device implanted instead of being brainwiped and banished to our prison society. Prevance said that he had been brainwiped and sterilized but that someone was needed to interface with the normal humans of the Universalist Council and he was evidently selected on the basis of some tests he took.

When the questioning of Prevance was finished, he was returned to a holding cell. The rest of us took a cokafa break before the questioning of Incate. Two VIS officers ushered Incate into the vericator room.

Incate was full of bluster and righteousness. He said, "You Delphs have no right to do this. I represent the Universalist Council. If you go against their wishes, there will be some changes around here."

Nordel replied, "There are certainly going to be changes around here. We're going to make them to aid us. The wishes of the Universalist Council are a matter of indifference to us. We see the Universalist Council as a group that has penalized us, imprisoned us, deceived us and exploited us. You should be concerned about what changes you, as an individual, will experience. You have come here under false pretenses. We know more of the truth than you suspect we do. If you continue to lie to us, you may lose more than you're willing to risk."

Incate seemed to lose some of his belligerence.

When the hookup was completed, Arvon began the questioning by asking, "What devices did you bring with you from the Outpost?"

Incate gave no response.

"Have you supplied spike mikes to Wanklurm?"

Evidently the question surprised Incate. He answered, "No, he got those from the Council." The monitor indicated he was telling the truth.

"Why was a non-possession device implanted in Prevance?"

"So the Council representatives could deal with him without fear of being possessed," Incate answered.

"Why wasn't a non-possession chip implanted in you?"

Incate was flustered by the question. He hadn't expected it. He fidgeted briefly and said, "What makes you think I don't have one?"

"We did a medical scan on you in the holding cell. You don't have any implants. We also know that your ejaculate, unlike that of the males here, contains sperm. Why is that? What is different about you?"

"Because I'm not one of *you*. I'm not some genetic reject who has to be imprisoned. I'm a normal. I have all those memories that you Delphs don't have. I remember growing up, getting educated, learning how to live. I would never have gotten this terrible assignment and had to mix with all you substandard types if I hadn't been falsely accused of excessive violence on my last case. Those smugglers were asking for it. Every last one of the five of them."

"You killed five smugglers?"

"They deserved it. Stealing human heritage artifacts to sell to collectors."

"Did you use a respirator arrestor?" Arvon asked.

"How did you know about that?"

"We assumed it's your favorite weapon since you had one concealed in your communication room in the House of Rebirth."

"It was for emergencies only." Incate said.

"And you are the one who decides whether or not an emergency situation exists."

"I'm qualified," he said smugly.

"We suspect that you are mainly qualified as an assassin. You were probably sent here to kill the conspirators, make sure their replacements would continue the deceptions of the Universalist Council, and get out before anyone with any power figured out what had been done."

Incate said nothing.

Arvon conferred with Nordel and Yondoka. Then Arvon said to the group, "Incate doesn't seem to be willing to answer questions but if anyone has any, now is the time."

"Why do you have so much hostility toward me?" I asked.

Incate answered, "Because you're one of these subhumans who are getting a free ride from the Universalist Council. Just because the Delphic data is needed, all of you get life easy."

I asked, "It's nothing personal, then?"

"No," he snarled. "I wish they'd sent me here with permission to kill all of you."

The monitor showed that he was telling the truth.

"You'd really be in trouble if all of us were dead."

"Why?"

"Because then you'd have no one to hate but yourself."

A few more questions were asked, but everyone soon tired of Incate's venom. As the VIS officers took him back to his holding cell, Incate said, "You'll regret this when I report this to the Council."

I couldn't resist the temptation to answer him. I said, "What makes you think you'll ever see the Council again or, that if you do, you will have any memory of what happened here?"

I didn't know what Incate's fate would be but I suspected that his fate would involve wiping his brain of the hate.

Lyonella and I went to the lounge. While we were sitting there, Kahalyton came by and said, "Come to the communications room if you want to hear the latest battle report."

It was a different VIS officer who reported the latest developments. He said, "The battle at Wanklurm's headquarters is over. Most of the building has been destroyed. Wanklurm and his few remaining elite guards have driven off the Crusaders. We aren't certain how many Crusaders are left alive but we know that Errox and his albino second-in-command Zuwelda, along with a handful of others, made a successful retreat and vanished. They've gone into hiding. Wanklurm and his guards are looking for them but haven't found them yet.

"We've got scouts in a variety of locations who'll report sightings of personnel from either the guards or the Crusaders. Medical Complex personnel are working to clear the area around Wanklurm's headquarters of bodies."

There were many questions. I heard all the answers but none of them gave me any clues to where Errox was. He had a rainbow wristlock which gave him access to almost any place he wanted to be. I doubted if he'd go to Dreena's dwell. By this time he probably knew that she had been arrested and was in a holding cell. I didn't think he'd try to regroup from Boget's dwell because for all he knew, it might still be under observation by watchers who hoped other conspirators might show up.

I was lost in thought when Lyonella touched my hand. She asked, "Is now the time we use my psychic link to find Errox?"

"Yes," I answered. "It's time to visit the Simulike Palace.
"

TWENTY-THREE

Although the fighting at Wanklurm's headquarters was over, most people still seemed to be staying in their urbodes where it was safe. No one knew where or when the few remaining guards and Crusaders would resume trying to kill each other. I wanted to find Errox and stop the mayhem if I could. All I had to offer Errox was a chance to live, although he would be brainwiped and reconfigured.

If Wanklurm and the guards found him his life would be ended by a bolt gun. I knew that Errox was a flawed human being, but he had saved my life once and I wanted to save him from death if I could.

The slideways were nearly deserted as Lyonella and I made our way to the Simulike Palace. When we got off, we both looked around carefully with our stun guns ready in case there were Crusaders acting as lookouts. We saw no one. As we got closer and closer to the building, I watched Lyonella to see if her psychic sense indicated that Errox was near. I thought that if she detected his presence she would give a positive nod. Instead she shook her head from side-to-side to show that she hadn't sensed him.

I got close enough to whisper in her ear, "Let's take a check inside. The public doorway is closed but my wristlock will open the private portal, the entrance for Palace personnel."

As I opened the portal I kept my stun gun ready, but I saw no one nearby. I entered first and Lyonella followed behind. I moved cautiously because Crusaders might be here even if Errox was not. I didn't have complete confidence in Lyonella's psychic connection to Errox. I knew that it had worked previously when I was in the corridor outside Hushel's previous dwell, but I couldn't be sure it was still working. Cainenol effects wore off with the passage of time; perhaps the same was true of psychic connections.

Slowly and carefully we checked out the entire building and found no evidence of anyone other than ourselves in the Palace. We both relaxed, our nerves stretched tight from the strain of the search.

Lyonella asked, "Where else would he go?"

"I don't know."

Lyonella said, "I first saw him when we had dwells in the same urbode. I never saw him anywhere except in an urbode. Where have you seen him?"

I thought about the various times I had seen Errox. I answered, "The last time I saw him was at Boget's dwell. Just before that I saw him at the dwell of Dreena the smitty. Before that I was here in the Simulike Palace with him until the VIS arrested me. Before Transit Day I saw him in the two dwells he found for me and in Hushel's dwell when he gave me his wristlock."

"Where did you first meet him?" she asked.

I must have been experiencing some sort of memory block that kept me from reviewing the details of my bad experiences of the Rainbow Room in the Color Wheel. I said, "It was at the Color Wheel. It's shut down now but he must have some way inside. He certainly knew the layout and he managed to get to the center of the Color Wheel, where the winner's circle is. I'm sure he didn't get there by taking chances in an environment where you risk your life."

"Let's try the Color Wheel, then," she suggested.

It was the most logical thing to do. I knew that I was resisting the idea because I didn't want to refresh the worst memories I had of this life. I finally agreed.

I spent the time on the slidestrips steeling myself for the unwanted sight of the Color Wheel. When it came into view, I felt nauseated. We got off the slideway using the Color Wheel access slidestrip. I took several deep breaths before I was ready to approach the building. This was the biggest challenge that I had faced in my life as Rathe, confronting the site where I had almost died.

I looked at the Color Wheel as if it were a dwell for my own private demons. I had to deal with the internal conflict to proceed.

Lyonella noticed that I was having difficulty. She asked, "Is there anything I can do to help?"

"I'll be all right. Let's go slowly. Tell me the moment you receive any indication that Errox is inside."

As we approached the Color Wheel we were careful to stay close to the surrounding buildings in case there were people watching. If Errox was there he might have posted a sentinel to warn him of anyone approaching.

When we got close enough to have a clear view of the closed public entrance, Lyonella said excitedly, "He's here!"

We had located Errox. I was as sure of it as I was of the bond between Lyonella and me. I said to Lyonella, "We need to notify the Alliance that Errox is here. I may be able to talk him into surrendering and ending this futile conflict. I can tell him that even if he defeats Wanklurm he'll never be able to rule the planet because the VIS people in the Alliance will stop him. If you're willing to take the news to the overseers' urbode so they can send some backup, I'll stay and watch to see if he leaves."

I don't know if Lyonella would have agreed to that plan or not because as the words left my mouth, we saw a group of about six white caps get off the slidestrip. I motioned to Lyonella to follow me and I lowered myself into the wide gutter that carried water away after the area was cleaned. When we were both horizontal we could peek over the edge of the gutter to watch the scene unfold. I recognized the man leading the white caps as Wanklurm, my first sighting of the man who had tried to have me killed and who would probably try again if the opportunity arose.

He and the white caps were all armed with bolt guns. Wanklurm posted one guard near the slidestrip apron. Then he and the others started moving toward the building. He was looking at something he held in his hand and walking toward the main portal of the Color Wheel. I realized that he was looking at a tracking device. Somehow he must have gotten a spike mike planted on Errox, maybe by turning a disgruntled or disillusioned Crusader into a supporter of the guards.

As Lyonella and I watched from our hiding place, Wanklurm used his rainbow wristlock to open the main entrance to the Color Wheel. Wanklurm gave some instructions to his guards that I couldn't quite hear and they all went in—all except the guard he'd left at the slidestrip exit. That guard represented a problem for Lyonella and me. How could we get a message to the overseers' urbode if we couldn't get past the guard to the slidestrip?

There was no way to get close enough to the guard to use a stun gun without him seeing us first. And if he saw us first, he might fire his bolt gun before we could stun him. Suddenly the lights came on in the Color Wheel. The outside building lights illuminated the gutter that Lyonella and I were hiding in. The guard near the slidestrip advanced toward us, his bolt gun in his hand aimed toward us.

"Come out of there with your hands up where I can see them," he ordered.

Knowing that we had no chance of stunning him before he could fire, Lyonella and I, as if by telepathic communication, both put our stun guns into our waist pouches before complying with the guard's order.

When we stood up, he asked, "What are you two doing here?"

Lyonella answered, "We were on our way to a jarva jump in the automatic factory session, when we saw some people with bolt guns. We got off the slidestrip and hid."

The guard asked, "Were those people Crusaders?"

Lyonella answered, "I don't know who they were."

"Were they wearing white caps?"

"No."

"Where did they go?"

"They went around the Color Wheel and then I couldn't see them anymore."

"All right. Both of you walk to the Color Wheel entrance. I'll be right behind you. If you try any tricks, you'll find out how fast I am with this gun."

We complied. My mind was churning out possible escape plans. None of them seemed feasible. I tried to remember everything I knew about the Color Wheel, hoping that something would suggest a plan. Kahalyton had told me that there was a choice of environments in the Color Wheel, all of them dangerous. I knew the dangers of the Rainbow Room but I knew nothing but the names of the other choices—the Mirror Maze, the Vibration Vessel, the Laser Lobby, the Hunting House, and the Bouncing Ballroom. I didn't know enough about those areas to make a plan.

I would have to be alert for any opportunity for us to escape. If we didn't, it was highly likely that my life would end here in the building where, as Rathe, my life began. Lyonella and I entered the building with the guard right behind us. As soon as we were inside he ushered us through an open access door with a smashed portal plate into a dimly lit, curved passageway with doors on both sides, doors that appeared to have no locking devices. I knew our guard was looking for Wanklurm and I was mentally searching for a way to avoid such a confrontation when we saw another guard ahead of us.

The man guarding us called out, "I've got two prisoners here. They were lurking around outside."

The guard ahead of us shouted, "Look out!"

We heard the thunder of a bolt gun followed immediately by the sound of the guard behind us falling to the floor.

As if we were one entity, Lyonella and I went through an unlocked door and found ourselves in a maze where all the surfaces were mirrors. We moved through the maze together putting distance between us and the killing in the corridor. The room was quiet except for our breathing. I listened for the thunder of bolt guns but didn't hear them. There were no mechanical sounds in this maze of mirrors. Evidently whatever life-threatening possibilities the room held were only activated when someone used a wristlock to enter as a contestant, someone who wanted to risk a life in the pursuit of an illusion.

Everywhere I looked I saw our reflections in the mirrors. Then I heard a bolt gun blast, followed by the sounds of mirrors cracking and broken glass falling. I grabbed Lyonella by the hand and we started running. I didn't know whether the shooter was an elite guard or a Crusader but I knew we had to get out of this room. Hoping that my sense of direction was accurate, I kept us moving toward the wall opposite the door through which we'd entered. The next shot of the bolt gun shattered the mirror directly before us, exposing an access door just like the one we'd used to enter. Lyonella and I dropped to the floor. We couldn't see the shooter. A second blast shook the door loose from its hinges.

We leaped up, ran through the door, and rushed down the curving corridor. We stopped running when we heard gunfire in the passageway. We looked for a way to escape.

The only door off this section of the corridor opened to our touch. We stepped in and the door slammed shut behind us. I looked around and saw familiar sights. We were in the Rainbow Room in the same spot where I had been dumped to die.

I felt panic stricken. I could feel my heart beat frantically.

Lyonella squeezed my hand. I took deep breaths and tried to calm my jabbering mind.

Lyonella asked, "Can you tell me what you see?"

"The seven colors of tiles. The display board. The door at the small end of the room."

Lyonella, in a very calm voice, said, "The tiles are stationary. The display board is blank. The door at the small end of the room is open."

She was right, panic had affected my senses. I shook myself as if to loosen the anxiety, took a deep breath, and said, pointing to the open door. "Beyond that door is the passageway that leads to the center of the Color Wheel. Let's move across the tiles as fast as we can and get through that door." We ran.

As soon as we got through the door I held Lyonella close to me and said, "I'll be all right now. I hope from here we can find a way out of the Color Wheel. Then we'll go to the overseers' urbode and report that both Errox and Wanklurm are here along with a few supporting troops, the ones who survived the headquarters battle."

To our right was an open portal marked with an encircled rainbow. I remembered it from my previous time here. It was the portal to the winner's circle. Perhaps there was an exit there. I put my finger against my lips to signal silence to Lyonella.

She nodded, showing that she understood.

I took the stun gun out of my waist pouch to be ready to deal with any Crusaders or guards with bolt guns. Lyonella was ready with her stun gun too. I was surprised as I looked into the winner's circle to see Errox sitting in a throne-like chair. His left arm was in a blood-stained sling. His left leg, partially wrapped in a bloody piece of tunic material, looked mangled, incapable of supporting his weight.

His right hand held a bolt gun that he was pointing straight ahead. He saw me but the gun never wavered. I took two steps forward to see his target. It was Wanklurm who was holding a bolt gun pointed at Errox. Errox glanced in my direction just long enough for Wanklurm to notice and say, "Welcome. You're just in time."

Wanklurm saw me, recognized me as Tannet, the man he'd tried to kill, and cried out, "You!"

As he focused the bolt gun on me, Lyonella and I fired our stun guns at the same instant. Wanklurm collapsed. Errox's bolt gun fired, too late to hit the stunned Wanklurm who had fallen to the floor. The noise of the bolt gun was followed by the sound of someone running.

Zuelda, the tall albino with the kinky hair who was Errox's second in command, entered the room in a rush with a bolt gun in her hand. There was a bandage around her head that covered one eye. She asked Errox, "Are you all right? I heard the gunfire."

"Yes. They stunned Wanklurm before he could kill me. My shot missed him."

If Errox recognized Lyonella he gave no indication of it. Errox looked at me and said, "Thanks for saving my life. We're even now."

Zuelda pointed her bolt gun at Wanklurm's chest and fired. The VIS commander's chest exploded with a spray of blood and gore.

She turned to Lyonella and me, "Thanks for stopping him from killing my lover. Who are you?"

She kept her bolt gun ready and kept shifting the focus of her one good eye between us and the door where someone might enter.

"Just two people who want to stop the fighting," I answered.

Errox put his bolt gun in his lap. With his right hand he reached into the container beside his chair and pulled out several multi-colored wristlocks. "I found the storage bin for removed wristlocks, the ones the winners turn in for new ones if they survive a visit to the Color Wheel. Now I can go into the wristlock business in a big way."

I wondered if his wound was affecting his thought processes. He had to have some idea of all the trouble he was in, even with Wanklurm dead.

Zuelda said, "There are only a few Crusaders and guards left. They are all someplace in the Color Wheel. We're here in the winner's circle, but there aren't going to be any winners today. The building is surrounded by VIS officers who are staying out of bolt gun range. Both the Crusaders and the white caps have lost. That last explosion at Wanklurm's headquarters wounded both of us. Even if we could escape from the guards and elude the VIS, we'd be captured as soon as we sought medical help."

Errox shook his head. "It isn't over yet."

Zuelda replied, "No, but it soon will be."

Then she looked first at Lyonella, then at me, and said, "There's a way out of here for you. I'll show it to you in appreciation for saving Errox."

She turned to Errox and said, "Hold on to your bolt gun and watch the door. I'll be right back."

She led us out of the winner's circle through a small passageway into a large sloping room with a chute at the lower end. It looked frighteningly familiar. She flipped a switch on the wall.

She said, "All will be ready soon. I'll have just enough time to get back and end the Crusade."

"How?" Lyonella asked.

"I'll fire the bolt gun into the container of wristlocks. They'll explode and destroy the entire building. Errox and I and all the other Crusaders will be reborn in the Free Land."

I realized that Zuelda was a true believer in the lies that Errox told about the Freedom Crusade. I knew there wasn't anything I could say that would change her mind. Instead, I asked, "How do we get out?"

Zuelda said, "Go to the far end, and wait by the chute. After I hear the water rush in, I'll set off the explosion."

She turned and left.

As Lyonella and I hurried toward the chute, I said, "I can't swim."

"I can," she said. "Just stay close to me."

We heard the boom of an explosion as the water rushed in and swept us away.

TWENTY-FOUR

A wave of water came like a returning nightmare and swept me away. I was better prepared for the ordeal this time. I kept my mouth closed, my head up, holding onto Lyonella. She was a skilled swimmer and steered us away from some of the walls I'd banged into before, although I did hit my head hard against some protrusion. We eventually reached a channel with shallow water, one we could stand up in as the current diminished.

We staggered to the bank, wet and dripping. We hugged each other, very glad to be alive even though we were somewhat battered and bruised.

The persistent hum in the air reminded me that we were in the automated factory section. When I had been here before, Errox had led the way out by a complex route that I had not been able to commit to memory. My mental map didn't include much about the autofactory areas. I asked Lyonella if she knew how to get to the overseers' urbode from here.

She said, "I know we're somewhere near the building where the drummers play. The nearest slidestrip isn't far but I think we should go to the Medical Complex first. The back of your head is bleeding and I think I have one or two broken ribs."

I held her gently and kissed the top of her head.

"We've got to tell the Alliance what happened," I said. "They don't know that Errox and Wanklurm are dead."

"They probably suspect that both of them were killed in the explosion. Zuelda said that VIS personnel had surrounded the Color Wheel."

I remembered Zuelda saying that and I wondered how the Alliance had learned where Errox and Wanklurm were. I asked Lyonella, "How do you think the Alliance found out where the Crusaders had gone?"

"I don't know but I'm sure we'll find out. Medical Complex first."

With Lyonella leading the way we went past a dozen or so of the large autofactories to the nearest slidestrip and got on. I pressed a piece of my ripped tunic against my head wound in an effort to reduce the bleeding. By the time we arrived at the Medical Complex I was shaky and weak from loss of blood. My eyes wouldn't focus right. I seemed to be experiencing double vision.

I passed out in the lobby.

*   *   *

When I returned to consciousness, I was on an individual sleep platform in unfamiliar surroundings and Lyonella was sitting beside me. A surge of joy went through me just to see her. I reached out to take her hand.

She said, "Welcome back. You suffered a concussion."

"How long have I been gone?"

"Several shifts."

"How are you?" she asked.

"I'm still sore, but my two cracked ribs are mending."

"Does the Alliance know what happened at the Color Wheel?"

"Yes. I reported what we witnessed. I also found out how the VIS learned that Errox was there. A scout saw Wanklurm using a tracking device and was sure that Crusaders were being tracked. She saw Wanklurm enter the Color Wheel and reported it to the VIS in the overseers' urbode."

"The fighting is all over?" I said, trying to keep my voice from shaking.

"Yes. Most of the Crusaders and guards who survived the battle at Wanklurm's headquarters were killed in the explosion. The survivors have been arrested. The Counter Colors have joined the Alliance. Together they've set up a temporary governing body to handle the transformation. Nobody knows what comes next, but it will be better than this false existence."

"What about the Universalist Council?"

"They haven't been informed of recent developments. Nordel and the rest of the governing body are planning to prepare a final report and deliver it to them along with the terms and conditions under which we are willing to continue supplying Delphic data. If you're feeling well enough there's a briefing meeting in the overseers' urbode after second meal."

"I'll be there," I said, "even if I have to be taken on a gurney."

The medics released me for the meeting. Lyonella and I held hands as we traveled the slideways. The world seemed like a better place to me, as if everything had been renewed, myself included. The briefing meeting was held in a large conference room in the overseers' urbode.

Kahalyton, Quenlu, Nordel, Yondoka, Clandine, Arvon, and many others were there along with some unfamiliar faces. I didn't see either Prevance or Incate. I wondered where they were.

Nordel opened the meeting by saying, "I'm delighted to see that Rathe is well enough to join us today. Speaking for all of us, I'd like to say how much we appreciate the efforts that he and Lyonella made to end the Crusader-guard conflict. Rathe and Lyonella, would you stand up please?"

Lyonella and I stood up to a burst of applause.

When the clapping began to fade, Nordel said, "Things are happening very fast, too fast for all of us to know all the details. I know that most of you have been too busy to know what some of the others have done or are in the process of doing so I'd like to summarize some of the high points.

"All of the people who conspired to distribute Cainenol are either dead or arrested. The survivors of the Crusader-elite guard conflict have been arrested. The VIS has been reorganized with a revised agenda under the dual leadership of Clandine and Arvon. The Color Wheel and Wanklurm's headquarters were destroyed. Both will eventually be replaced with something more appropriate to our needs, probably education centers. The House of Rebirth remains closed to shipments of human beings from the Universalist Council; the Council will be notified that we will no longer accept brainwiped humans from the Universalist worlds under any circumstances. Later on we will develop immigration policies and procedures but the ban on brainwiped individuals will continue.

"The Universalists will have to find another way to deal with the possession problem such as machines that block the signal like our tide machines do or by the implantation of micro-devices like the one implanted in Prevance."

When Nordel said that he glanced toward the rear of the room. I looked around and saw Prevance sitting in the back row. Incate was not with him.

Nordel continued. "One of the areas we want the Council to explore is medical research. If they can find a way to alter the possession genes then they can eliminate the problem on all their worlds. They need to recognize that they can't use our world as a depository for the citizens they find undesirable."

Nordel paused, coughed, and then said, "We are making progress in a number of areas. The Simulike Palace is operating with the new machines. Some of the technical people from the Counter Colors are converting the output to input data for our Game players to use in helping map out our future. We think that a large sample of future Simulike experiences will alert us to possibilities and probabilities as well as some pitfalls that can be avoided.

"Rathe was the person who suggested this approach and we want him on that team as soon as he is recovered from his injury. The Game players have been told the nature of the Game. Most of them want to continue, if we reach agreement with the Universalist Council as to what we will receive in exchange for the Delphic data we create. What we will want in exchange will be whatever we need to transform the culture into one that serves our needs rather than the needs of the Universalists.

"The Clergy Guild has been abolished because the religious framework in which the clerics operated did little, if anything, to aid individuals. We are working on a plan to combine the clergy and listener functions in a system that is logical and practical without requiring belief in anything that can't be proved. Lyonella is working on this project and has assured me she is ready to accept input from anyone who has thoughts on the subject. I'd like to call on Kahalyton now to brief us on other developments."

We applauded Nordel.

Then Kahalyton, the sage from my Simulike experience, took the floor. "Quenlu and Yondoka have told all the storytellers what has happened. The storytellers will reveal this to their audiences and ask them to spread the news. Machines that remove and defuse wristlocks will be universally available before next Transit Day, when changing dwells becomes a matter of choice rather than a rigid requirement. All the dwell portal plates that opened to wristlocks will be changed to open to the resident's palm print.

"Any or all of the mechanisms that make this society self-supporting can be reprogrammed by our technical people to meet our needs. We intend to set up teaching programs for anyone who wants to learn how things work. There are a lot of other projects in progress or under consideration."

Kahalyton sat down to the sound of clapping hands. I was pleased that this dynamic person was part of the coming cultural change.

Nordel took the floor, saying: "Perhaps some of you are wondering what has happened to the few people we placed under arrest. All of them except one have been brainwiped and reconfigured. They will be re-educated and brought back into our society. The one exception is the off-world investigator Incate. Under the rules established by the Universalists that were in effect when Incate arrived, he is guilty of a number of offenses:

"One: introducing new weapons; he brought in a respirator arrestor that has been destroyed. Two: personal misrepresentation; he claimed to have the possession genes but he does not. Three: hampering an official investigation by withholding information; he didn't reveal his knowledge of the underlying problems that created the situation he was investigating. Universalist rules say that three or more offenses require the offender to be brainwiped. We felt that applied to everyone so Incate has been brainwiped.

"He has not been reconfigured because he doesn't have the genetic requirement to be a member of our current society. He will be returned to the Universalists by our ambassador to the Council."

The question that immediately popped into my mind was: Who would be the ambassador? Who was qualified to deal with the Universalists, the complexities, the issues, the many unknowns as we established ourselves as an independent human settlement?

Nordel answered my unspoken question. "I propose that Prevance be nominated as our ambassador to the Universalist Council. He is the only one among us who has experience with the Universalists. He has the implanted computer chip that blocks the operation of the possession gene. He can be one of us and yet walk among the Universalists without arousing the specter of possession. In the time that Prevance has been here, he, unlike Incate, has shown understanding, compassion, intelligence, truthfulness, and a willingness to do his best. I think he is a great choice for ambassador but I will open the floor for other nominations."

When no one spoke up, Nordel said, "Since there are no other nominations I would like Prevance to make an acceptance speech."

Prevance came forward. "I'll make this short. I wanted the job. I'm glad I got it. I'm going to do the best I can for all of us. I intend to persuade the Council that they must make efforts to find a better solution to the possession problem than the deceitful culture they created here. As we create a new society we must improve communication and education. The Universalists are all literate. They can read and write.

"This knowledge has been forbidden by making sure that no reading material was sent here and the previous regulations considered any writing to be a desecration offense. However, we all have the ability to read and write."

When Prevance said that, I realized that I had read the numbers on the Rainbow Room display without difficulty. I could read and write, too! The Universalists had created this culture without providing any reading material, writing implements, or other products that would make us aware of this ability. Their actions had limited our ability to communicate, but that would change.

Prevance continued. "This untapped potential for communication has been verified in our educational workshop. The brainwiping did not flush that out of our minds. We are going to identify all buildings, slideways and slidestrips with names and numbers so that everyone will be able to move freely without having to construct a mental map. I came to this world as a stranger, having no idea what it was like to live in a society designed to exploit and control the entire population while keeping them in ignorance. The more I saw, the more I realized change was necessary. I'm proud to be part of that change. Thank you."

We all applauded and Nordel ended the meeting.

People conversed in small groups. Everyone was excited about the changes that were underway and the future possibilities of an open, honest society.

After we'd spoken with friends and acquaintances, Lyonella turned to me, saying, "You were just released from the Medical Complex. You mustn't tire yourself out. You're supposed to rest frequently. Why don't we retire to our dwell for a nap?"

A thrill shot through me when she said "our dwell." I looked at Lyonella and was overwhelmed by feelings of love, affection, tenderness, and desire.

I said, "You and I have been through a lot of changes and there are more changes to come. I want us to face the future together as a team of two."

Lyonella looked at me in a way that made my heart melt and said, "I want that, too."

She took me by the hand and led me to our dwell. Inside we had our own private ceremony in which we vowed to stay together, to treat each other well and love each other as best we could. I said, "I've got a lot to learn about commitment."

She said, "We'll learn together."

"There are things you'll have to teach me."

Lyonella asked, "Would you like for me to make a list?"

I said, "If you do, be sure to include teaching me to swim."

The End